Before I can think any more about it, I lean into him and press my lips to his. I kiss him like I actually know what I'm doing. Like I've thrown myself at dozens of guys before—or, better yet, like dozens of them have thrown themselves at me. He's startled, but only for a second, and then he responds, cupping the back of my head while his other arm tightens against my back.

With my brain still zinging around in the stratosphere, I pull back. "For luck."

Also by Liz Czukas

*Ask Again Later*

# TOP TEN CLUES YOU'RE CLUELESS

LIZ CZUKAS

HARPER TEEN
An Imprint of HarperCollinsPublishers

HarperTeen is an imprint of HarperCollins Publishers.

Top Ten Clues You're Clueless
Copyright © 2014 by Liz Czukas

Library of Congress Cataloging-in-Publication Data
Czukas, Liz.
    Top ten clues you're clueless / Liz Czukas. — First edition.
        pages  cm
    Summary: The day before Christmas, money goes missing from a donation box
at GoodFoods Market and Chloe and her five teenage coworkers, held in the
break room until the police arrive, try to identify the real thief.
    ISBN 978-0-06-227242-3 (pbk.)
    [1. Grocery trade—Fiction. 2. Interpersonal relations—Fiction. 3. Lists—
Fiction. 4. Stealing—Fiction. 5. Christmas—Fiction. 6. Mystery and detective
stories.] I. Title. II. Title: Top ten clues you are clueless.
PZ7.C9993Top 2014                                                    2013051290
[Fic]—dc23                                                                  CIP
                                                                            AC

Typography by Torborg Davern
14 15 16 17 18  LP/RRDH  10 9 8 7 6 5 4 3 2 1

First Edition

*To sallie, who believed*

# TOP TEN WEIRDEST THINGS PEOPLE DO EVERY DAY AT GOODFOODS MARKET

10. Try to pay for their stuff with stolen credit cards and then get pissed off when we have to cut the cards up.

9. Leave frozen foods—especially ice cream—in the nonfreezer sections, so they melt all over everything.

8. Try to do that extreme couponing stuff just because they've seen a couple episodes of that TV show.

7. Try to get refunds on food they didn't like. After they ate it.

6. Let their kids run around the store like it's a playground, then get all panicky when their little precious darlings get lost.

5. Come in on Saturdays and eat enough samples to make a meal.

4. Think that it's perfectly acceptable to make out in the aisles or the bathrooms.
3. Insist on only buying produce "from the back" even when we've got the freshest stuff out already and the stuff from the back is visibly rotting.
2. Try to return partially eaten cakes, claiming they're too dry.
1. Eat food while they're in the store, then stuff the empty boxes and bags behind other food on the shelf.

I had to get up before the sun today, so I can't really be held responsible for the fact that I hit the snooze button three times. Fatal mistake. Everything was dependent on me getting up on time. It's never a good sign when you wake up screwed.

I went to sleep with damp hair and now half my head looks like it's been ironed, while the other half looks like I stuck my finger in a light socket. A ponytail is the only solution. My favorite jeans are nowhere to be found, and my festive Christmas socks turn out to have holes in the toes.

This is not what I had in mind for this morning. Especially since everyone at GoodFoods has been telling me for weeks that today is going to kick my butt. Christmas Eve is one of the busiest shopping days of the year, and grocery stores are no exception.

I'm running late, of course, so I shouldn't stop for anything, but there are some things that just cannot be skipped. For me, that's today's list.

My list habit started in fifth grade. My best friend, Eva, and I wrote each other notes every night. As we got older, they turned into daily to-do lists. The thing was, we wrote them for each other. Sometimes there were simple tasks on the lists, like, "Get through biology class today without falling asleep." Sometimes, they were closer to dares, like, "Finally talk to Connor Richards."

Since my family moved, though, Eva and I don't go to the same school. And she doesn't write me lists anymore. She doesn't really keep in touch at all, actually. Not even a Like on Facebook. Of course, my status updates lately haven't exactly been the stuff of legend: *Off to work!* and *Ugh, I hate Mondays.*

Try not to faint with excitement.

Once Eva dropped out of my life, I started writing my own lists. Daring myself to not be the clichéd New Kid who doesn't fit in. So far, it's not working. Like, at all.

I know—it's so nerdy, right? I keep hearing that being a geek is cool now, but I'm not sure the rest of the world has gotten the memo, because I still feel like a pretty big dork compared to a lot of people at my new school. And being insecure makes me want to write more lists, which makes me feel nerdier, which makes me write more lists. . . . You can see my problem.

My mom says list making is "a good habit I'll be grateful for in my future career." Then again she's the kind of person who labeled her label maker with a label that says "Label Maker," so I'm not sure she's the world's most trustworthy authority on good habits. My older brother, David, says someday the wrong person is going to see one of my lists and I'm going to get burned, but most of my lists are too boring for anyone to bother reading, much less use against me. Besides, I've solved that problem by not really making any friends yet, so no one even knows about my lists, much less tries to read them.

Which brings me to today's list.

## TO-DO, 12/24

1. Talk to at least three of my coworkers long enough to learn something new about them.
2. Try not to let my mouth take over my brain during those conversations.
3. Actually remember to turn off my ringer when I get to work.
4. Write no more than three lists during the day.

5. Pick up the Christmas ham Mom ordered from the butcher department.
6. Give Tyson a ride home.

So maybe not every day can be action-packed.

As I tuck my little notebook into my back pocket, I glance at the clock and see I'm going to be seriously late if I don't get in the car in the next two minutes. Crap. And there's still the possibility of running into my mother, which will only make me later. Please, God, let her still be asleep! I grab my shoes and do my best to run silently down the stairs.

"Chloe."

I let out a choked scream, my hand flying up to cover my mouth, cracking myself in the cheekbone with my shoes as a result. So much for stealth. I have no idea how she snuck up on me like that. Some kind of secret Mom-ninja skill.

"I thought I'd get started early and drive you to work," she says brightly, unaware she almost made me wet myself.

My heart is slowing from the scare, but now a dash of annoyance flits through my system, zinging my pulse back up a few notches. "Why? It's Christmas Eve."

"Exactly." My mother takes a couple steps forward and

I can see her more clearly.

I notice she's already dressed in a Christmas sweater and dangly earrings that look like tiny Christmas ornaments. Makeup, too, I think, though it's hard to be certain with the twinkling of the multicolored LED lights out on the front porch, which means she got up early enough to not only be completely made up, but turn on the twinkle lights.

Yikes.

This is officially Christmas overdrive. Maybe it's the new house that's made her go Christmas bonkers, or maybe it's my brother coming home from college for the first time. Either way, my mother is going to need a twelve-step program to detox from her insane holiday prep routine this year.

But back to the matter at hand.

"It's no big deal, Mom."

"You shouldn't have to drive all by yourself on Christmas Eve!" she says.

"But if you drive me, how am I supposed to get home after my shift?" I prop one hand on the wall and bring a foot up to shove my shoe on.

"I'll come back and get you." She gives me a hopeful smile.

"In the middle of the afternoon? With David coming home?"

My mom purses her lips, trying to think of a way to baby me and my brother simultaneously. She is the undisputed master of babying.

I jump in before she can suggest a do-it-yourself wormhole or something. "I really don't mind, Mom. Besides, it'll save gas, right? And you don't want to be gone when David gets here, do you?" Maybe if I keep using my brother's name over and over she'll redirect her energy to him.

"But the weather . . ." Her lower lip disappears between her teeth, her signature worry gesture.

"I'll be okay. You should be here when David gets home."

And if I don't have my car, there is no way that Tyson Scott will ask for a ride home. And if Tyson doesn't ask me for a ride home . . . well, then I can't give him one, can I? And it's on the list, after all. That makes it practically ordained.

She's eyeing me critically, with a certain glint that tells me she's still trying to figure out how to emerge the winner. I stay resolute, certain this time there is no magical Mom solution. Finally, she drawls, "I suppose. But at least let me get you breakfast."

"No time. I'll be late."

The warm and fuzzy Christmas Mom is gone in an instant. "Chloe."

Yeah, I should have seen that coming. If there is one thing my mother won't tolerate, it's me playing roulette with my diabetes. I was diagnosed with type I when I was three, and she's pretty much been a complete spaz about what, when, where, and how much I eat ever since.

I'm what is referred to as a "brittle" diabetic, which always makes me feel like I might be made of glass, but actually means that my blood sugars don't stay well controlled. No matter how carefully I watch what I eat and how precisely we time the insulin, I can still sometimes make big yo-yoing changes without warning. My mom regards this as a personal attack, and she has vowed revenge on the evil pancreas that enslaves her daughter. I should get her a Viking helmet.

"All right, all right." Opening the refrigerator, I snag one of the disgusting Glucerna drinks we keep around in case of emergency and grab a banana from the counter. Looking back at my mother, I see how worried she looks, and guilt pinches at me. "Sorry, Mom. If I'd gotten up earlier . . ."

"You need more protein than that," she says, opening

the refrigerator and pulling out two slices of deli turkey.

"Really?" I ask with a sigh. One of these days, I'm going to turn into a person-shaped sculpture of deli-sliced turkey. It's nearly instant, low-fat protein. The pediatric dietician told my parents about it when I was first diagnosed, and since then, my mom has shoved it at me whenever she thinks I haven't eaten enough. I shudder to think how many turkeys have given their lives in the name of my defective pancreas.

"There's no time for a real breakfast. You said so yourself."

"Okay." I take the cold cuts and tuck them both into my mouth at once, chewing madly. I barely taste them before they're gone.

"Thank you." She smiles. "And take this, too." She lifts a paper bag off the counter. She packed me a lunch.

Part of me wants to knock it away—remind her that I'm going to work in a giant building literally full of food—but it's Christmas Eve and I already know how this story ends. Spoiler alert: the mom always wins.

So, I grit my teeth and say, "Thank you."

She looks relieved. "You're welcome. Take care of yourself."

"I will, Mom."

With her paranoia extinguished, I zip my jacket and scoop up my ad hoc breakfast once more.

"Merry Christmas Eve, honey!" my mom calls after me.

Outside, the sky is even darker than it should be, given the hour. There are heavy clouds overhead. The air feels damp, but even though it's cold, it's too warm for snow. Definitely not the kind of White Christmas people dream about.

The passenger door on my ugly teal Chevy Malibu is frozen shut, so I have to use the key to break through the ice, and then brace my foot against the car to yank the door open. If only the lock on the driver's side worked— it's downwind and wouldn't be shellacked in ice. My brother swears up and down there is a trick to opening it, but after driving the car for five months, I still can't get it. I always have to crawl across the front seat to get behind the wheel.

The leg of my jeans catches on the parking brake and I spend another precious minute unhooking myself. My glasses slide so far down my nose I can't see straight, and I'm in such an awkward position I have to hold the steering wheel with one hand and try to balance on the opposite knee while my left hand searches for the tangled threads. Finally, I just yank, and the ripping sound that follows tells me the hem is torn. As a bonus, I lose my balance and bump my head on the headrest.

"Stupid snooze button," I mutter as I back out of the driveway.

Six a.m. is an inhumane time to start working. I don't usually work the opening shift, but with the crowds we're expecting and the shortened day, practically every employee is scheduled this morning. My eyes burn and itch from being open hours too early. I'm still trying to scrub the sleep out of them—one at a time of course, because I'm driving—when the GoodFoods Market sign comes into view.

At the far end of the parking lot, a city bus is pulling away. My heart starts beating a little faster, because I know who takes the bus to work.

And there he is.

Tyson.

Even with his heavy black coat on, and the hood pulled up over his head, I can tell it's him.

I steer my car into the lot and cut across the empty painted parking stalls to pull into one of the spots around the side of the building reserved for employees. Tyson is still only halfway across the lot when I get out of my car. I should have driven a little slower because now I have to make a decision: To wait, or not to wait?

## REASONS TYSON SCOTT IS WORTH WAITING FOR IN A FREEZING PARKING LOT

1. When he smiles, you can't help smiling back.
2. His dark brown eyes. Completely gorgeous even when partially hidden behind glasses, which incidentally make him look handsome and intelligent.
3. He drops everything to help old ladies get their bags loaded into their cars.
4. The way he can't help grooving along to the music that plays on the speaker system. (Except at Christmas, because nobody can groove to "Here Comes Santa Claus.")
5. He has never once called me a nerd, even when I spent an entire shift telling him about the special I watched on the Science Channel on forensics, because I don't know how to shut up, even when I really, really should.
6. We have spent more than one shift talking about Harry Potter, and he once admitted to me that he spent his entire eleventh birthday waiting for an owl to arrive.

Now if only I could tell whether he actually wanted *me* to wait for him in a freezing parking lot.

I try to convince my feet to move and take me inside,

but it doesn't work. I just stand there like a statue of indecision with the cold seeping up through the soles of my shoes.

Just then, I hear the first *chi-ching chi-ching chi-ching* of the Salvation Army bell ringer from the front of the building. My ears recoil at the sound. I've been hearing it for nearly two months now, and it's become like a headache in audible format. What kind of overenthusiastic volunteer is here ringing the bell before the store is open?

I glance across the parking lot at Tyson, who makes an exaggerated point at the front of the building and mimes ringing a bell before shaking his head. I laugh, sending a plume of frozen breath up in the heavy air. He's close. Close enough that it's not weird if I wait for him anymore. Especially since we're practically having a conversation, right?

He slows as he reaches me, his sneakers slapping the ground with a strange, clangy echo in the cold.

"Hey, Chloe! Merry Christmas!" He's breathing hard.

"Merry Christmas *Eve*." Why did I do that? I think my mother's obsession with the holiday has finally affected me.

Tyson just laughs, though. "Come on. We don't want to be late. Agnes might tell on us."

I pretend to shake in fear. "You're right, we better hurry."

Tyson yanks on the employee entrance door and stands to the side. "After you."

So, so courteous. I should add that to the list.

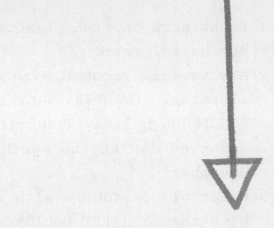

MEMO–MEMO–MEMO–MEMO–MEMO–MEMO–MEMO

TO: ALL EMPLOYEES SCHEDULED TO WORK
DECEMBER 24

As you know, Christmas Eve is one
of the biggest shopping days of
the year. We anticipate this year
will be particularly busy due to
in-store promotions.

Employees are expected to adhere
to and exceed the usual code of
conduct.

1. Be at work on time. Tardiness will not be tolerated!
2. Arrive well groomed with clean clothing. REMINDER: Your red GOODFOODS holiday T-shirts are required during the month of December.
3. Greet all customers with a smile. Wish them a HAPPY HOLIDAYS when your transactions are complete.
4. There is no such thing as "downtime." If you are not busy at your assigned task, FIND SOMETHING TO DO! There are always carts to be collected, shelves to be fronted, and general cleaning to be done. If you need help finding a task, ASK!
5. District Manager Gene Solomon will be at the store to collect the money from our Holiday Donation Box. Please assist him in any way he requires.
6. Local media will be here for the presentation of the check to Full

Hearts Full Plates. Greet them
enthusiastically and smile for the
camera. This is a big day for the
store!
7. There will be Christmas cookies
and eggnog available in the
employee Break Room. Please limit
yourself to one cookie and one
small cup of eggnog.

Happy Holidays!
Your Management Team

Just inside the door, I pause as the temperature change
makes condensation collect on my glasses. Tyson leans
toward me and says, "Man, I hate it when they fog," with
a grin. I have to look over the tops of my own steamed-up
lenses to see that his have gone opaque, too.

"Right?" I agree. I don't usually mind wearing glasses—
not to mention my innate fear of touching my eyes that
prevents me from making the switch to contacts—but
coming in from the cold and having a moment of tempo-
rary blindness always makes me wonder if it's really worth
resigning myself to a lifetime of this.

Tyson does a silly pantomime of grappling through the dark, which I can barely see through my own fog, but I laugh anyway. After a moment the haze clears and I can take in the view.

The Break Room is crowded with more GoodFoods employees than I've ever seen in the store before. A lot of people are clutching cups of coffee like life preservers. A few spare a moment to nod, or mumble hellos as Tyson and I move through the room toward the bank of small lockers.

A couple of times, he puts one hand on my back to steer me through the crowd. Even through my thick winter coat, I swear I can feel heat from his hand. Or maybe that heat is coming from inside me. Either way, I like the feeling of it, even when it starts to spread toward my cheeks in a secret-telling blush.

Our lockers aren't right next to each other, but they're close enough that it's hard for us both to use them at the same time. Of course, Tyson gestures for me to go first, but I shake my head.

"No, you first. Please." I flatten one hand in an "after you" gesture.

He looks ready to double up on chivalry, but I smile and nod encouragingly and he gives in. This is exactly what I was hoping for, because when he turns his back, I yank my can of Glucerna out of my coat pocket and toss it in the big gray garbage can nearby.

THINGS I WOULD RATHER DRINK THAN GLUCERNA
1. Coffee with no cream or Splenda.
2. Well water.
3. Pickle juice.
4. Clamato juice.
5. The water left over after boiling noodles.

When Tyson is done, he steps aside and makes a slight bow toward me. I cram my coat into the little cube, wondering for the millionth time why they couldn't give us larger lockers. These aren't even as big as the kind you can rent for a quarter at the mall. I manage to get the door shut with my coat and my brown-bag lunch inside, and secure it with my combination lock.

"Ready to see what the day has in store for us?" Tyson asks, nodding toward the assignment board mounted on the far wall.

"You betcha." I cringe inwardly as I start moving toward the other side of the room. *Couldn't go with a simple yes, huh?* I ask myself.

The giant whiteboard with all the job assignments takes up most of the wall, but it's so covered with info, you have to be close to see it well. I squeeze between two of the lunch tables to get a good view, and scan for my name. There it is, next to register number six. Tyson's listed under the baggers for the day. The baggers rotate among the registers and some of the other front work, like cart collecting and carrying out packages. There's no reason to think he'll be my bagger, but I cross my fingers down at my side anyway.

Then I check who's assigned to the registers on lanes five and seven.

Agnes is on seven. Ugh.

Agnes, as far as anyone can tell, has been working at GoodFoods since before the building was constructed. One of the other guys who works here, Gabe, says they must have built it around her. She seems to be about ninety years old, but somehow she has enough energy to do more than anyone else and make the rest of us feel guilty about not performing at the same level. It's like the worst super-power ever.

Case in point, she is currently wiping down every sur-face in here with antibacterial wipes. More than likely, she worked until closing last night and disinfected the whole room before she left, too. You could probably do surgery in here.

So who's on lane five? Zaina. My thumbnail finds its way between my teeth before I can stifle the habit. Zaina's about my age, I think, though she hasn't talked to me enough to confirm it. It's not just me; she doesn't talk to anyone very much.

## THE TINY BIT OF INFORMATION I'VE BEEN ABLE TO GATHER ABOUT ZAINA

1. She's in high school.
2. She wasn't born in the US, but I don't know where she's from and I haven't figured out how to ask, even though I'm dying to know.
3. She is the most beautiful human being I've ever seen in real life. This is not an exaggeration. She's so beautiful that I've seen people forget what they're supposed to do when they get up to her register.
4. She's very quiet.
5. Kris, my favorite of the shift managers, calls her Z, so it's possible this is her nickname.

At least she's better than Agnes.

It's funny how circumstances can dictate your level of excitement about the people around you. Like, at school, the only people you want to see are your closest friends. If you have a class with no friends in it, you might as well be sentenced to prison. But if you were at some kind of outside event, and there was even one person from your school there and everyone else was an adult, you'd be instant BFFs. For a little while.

Anyway, my point is that Zaina and I aren't exactly tight, but compared to Agnes, she might as well be my long-lost sister.

"Looks like all the Younglings are on today," Tyson says near my ear, sending goose bumps racing along my spine. I didn't realize he was still so close.

"Yeah?" Younglings is what Kris calls all the high-school kids who work at the store. There aren't many of us—six, to be exact—and it's rare for us to all be on at the same time. I take another look at the assignment board:

Tyson Scott—bagger, front jobs
Zaina Malak—cashier, lane 5
Micah Yoder—swing stocker
Gabe Rossi—swing cashier
Sammi Baker—swing bagger

And of course there's me on lane six.

In the upper left corner, I also note that Kris is our shift manager for the day. Thank God. If what everyone has been saying is true, today is going to be crazy. Kris is the only sane and laid-back person from management.

As if my thoughts made him appear, Kris's voice booms across the Break Room.

"Younglings!" He looks entirely too alert for this awful hour of the morning. I have an instinct to shield my eyes from his cheerful glow.

"Morning, Kris," Tyson says.

"Happy holidays," I add.

"Right. Ho ho ho and all that." Kris gives us a big, cheesy smile. "So, my young ones, what is happening?" He turns his head as he talks to include Micah, Sammi, and Gabe, who arrived in his wake.

"It's too damn early for your cheerfulness, Kris." Sammi levels him with a glare over the lid of her coffee cup.

"Your predictable snarkiness is adorable, Sammi." Kris makes as if to pinch her cheek, and Sammi pulls away with a nasty look.

Kris laughs. "I know it's early, but come on, it's Christmas Eve! You can't be crabby on Christmas Eve."

"Sammi can be crabby anywhere, anytime," Gabe says. "It's her gift."

She gives Gabe a look, but it's more "ha-ha, you think you're so funny" than "die, mortal scum." Gabe's usually the only one who earns the former.

"Should I go out and clear the walks?" Micah fiddles with the zipper on his jacket.

Gabe groans. "Seriously? You're asking for extra work?"

"It *is* a job," Sammi reminds him.

"Yeah, but that doesn't mean you have to volunteer for shoveling."

"I don't mind!" Micah smiles.

And I totally believe him, because he's Micah. Straw-blond hair, blue eyes, always smiling. He looks like one of those statues of children with big heads hugging puppies or kneeling for prayers. He should have an actual halo floating over his head.

"I love this kid." Kris thumps Micah on the shoulder, then claps his hands twice, hard. The sound clangs in my ears. "All right, people." His voice is loud enough to silence the mutterings of the rest of the people in the room. "We have a hell of a busy day ahead of us. Let's just try to get through this as quickly and easily as we can, mmmkay?"

I hear a small huff near the punch-in clock and catch a brief look of annoyance from Agnes. Her disapproval for Kris beams from her pores.

"You gonna give us our tills, or what?" Gabe asks Kris, nodding toward the Count Out room, where all the money trays are locked up overnight.

"Ha. You wish. Go grab a shovel and get to work on the walks with Micah. You too, Tyson."

Sammi cackles as she hoists her coffee cup to her lips once more. "Burn."

"Aw, man." Gabe scowls. "I hate shoveling."

"I don't mind," Micah pipes up again.

"Of course you don't." Gabe sighs.

"Micah, if I asked you to go up on the roof to check for ice damming, would you do it?" Kris asks.

Micah's eyes go wide. "Do you want me to?"

"No, I was just wondering."

"Well, sure, if you needed me to."

Sammi shakes her head. "Unbelievable. I'm leaving before I get involuntarily turned into an Eagle Scout."

Kris nods to me. "Come on, Red. Let's get you and Z your drawers."

Zaina is still exactly where I last saw her, waiting. I look at the lockers where Tyson is shrugging back into his coat to go out on shoveling duty. He doesn't notice me looking, though, so there are no sudden declarations of love on his part.

I know. Weird, right?

Just then the overhead speakers click loudly and the ubiquitous Christmas music starts. The first selection of the day? "Here Comes Santa Claus."

Guess it's officially time for work.

MY FIVE LEAST-FAVORITE CHRISTMAS CAROLS THAT
I USED TO THINK WERE OKAY BEFORE WORKING IN
A STORE THAT PLAYED THEM NONSTOP FOR TWO
STRAIGHT MONTHS

1. "Feliz Navidad"
2. "The Christmas Shoes"
3. "My Grown-Up Christmas List"
4. "Old Saint Nick"
5. "Last Christmas"

The trouble with "Feliz Navidad" is that everyone hates it, but you can't stop yourself from singing it. Every single time it comes through the sound system, I cringe, and then half a verse later, I'm humming along.

So that's what I'm doing while I key in the code for my

customer's giant bag of limes. It's hard to imagine what a small blond woman could do with that many limes. I've worked at GoodFoods for almost nine months, and I still haven't lost my fascination with the things people buy. I make lists of the weirdest combos I encounter every time I work.

This woman is definitely going on the list. She looks about thirty years old, no wedding ring on her finger, no kids in her cart. It's Christmas Eve, and she's bothered to come to the store for a bag of limes—nearly twenty, I'd guess—a box of Bisquick, a small jar of cinnamon, and hand soap.

"... *prospero año y felicidad* . . . ," I sing softly as I steeple my fingers over the receipt printer. I hand it off to the blonde and wish her a happy holiday. She doesn't respond, which only adds to her mysteriousness. Most people can't override that reflex to reply.

I check my watch, automatically doing the calculation in my head for how long it's been since I've eaten, when I'll need to eat again, and what level my insulin pump is running at. I'm in the safe zone, by my quick math, which is good, because I keep my insulin pump clipped to my bra while I'm at work, so it's not exactly accessible if I need to make any adjustments. My first couple shifts, I kept it on my waistband, like usual, but I bumped into the register a few times and accidentally gave myself an extra dose of insulin. It's easier to keep it hidden and out of reach. Plus, this way no one asks me about it.

I'm not ashamed of being diabetic or anything; it's just nice to have some people in my life who don't stare at me while I eat. Or don't eat. Or if I get a little sweaty when it's hot out. Or if I look a little pale under fluorescent lighting.

Not that my mother has tried my patience on this or anything.

"Hello! Did you find everything you were looking for today?" I ask my next customer, a man who is clearly on a mission to the store from his wife. As a rule, men don't buy heavy whipping cream and whole cloves.

"Put it in paper" is all he says.

So much for the holiday spirit. I turn to call down to the end of the register. "He'd like paper, please."

Tyson—he did get assigned to my lane!—nods and reaches for the stack of paper bags.

The guy doesn't speak another word to me or Tyson, even though Tyson is superfriendly. Some people are such jerks.

My next customer has a big order, so I know I'll have a few minutes of mindless scanning.

"What are you doing for Christmas?" I ask Tyson.

"Family stuff." He shrugs. "My grandma and aunties have been cooking for days already."

"Yeah?" I can't help smiling. There's something adorable about the way he calls them his aunties. He was born in the South, and sometimes there's a sweet twang to his words. "My mom's been in Christmas overdrive this year, too. It's my brother's first year at college, and she wants it to be all special and stuff, especially since he couldn't come home for Thanksgiving because he went to see his girlfriend's family. Still, I'm not sure it's actually a legitimate reason to go Christmas crazy, since it's not like he's been gone all that long, and it's not like he said he wasn't going to come home or something—" I'm babbling. I can hear it myself. Never a good sign.

I swear, I must be missing some crucial part in my brain that tells my mouth to stop moving.

Tyson is nodding, though, and he looks like I might even be saying something interesting. Is that possible?

"Excuse me," a voice says rather sharply, and I startle out of my motormouth trance. It's my customer, and from the look on her face, it's not the first time she tried to get my attention.

"Yes?" My whole head goes hot with embarrassment.

# TOP TEN THINGS THAT SUCK ABOUT BEING A REDHEAD

10. I blush the color of a tomato in an instant.

9. I have never gotten a suntan a day in my life.

8. I have had plenty of sunburns. Wicked nasty, peeling, blistering sunburns.

7. There is no shade of makeup that matches "pasty bluish white and covered in freckles."

6. Same goes for pantyhose, bandages, fake-tanning spray, and all other so-called flesh-toned items.

5. Everyone asks if this is my natural color.

4. Perverts ask if the carpet matches the drapes.

3. The carpet matches the drapes.

2. People call me Red or Little Orphan Annie, like they're the first people who ever thought of that.

1. People assume I'm Irish, and therefore that I love Saint Patrick's Day.

"I said there's a broken egg in this carton and I need a different one."

"Oh. Right." I nod, wishing I could spontaneously unblush. "Um . . ."

"I'll get it," Tyson says cheerfully. He squeezes past her cart and holds out his hand for me to give him the faulty carton.

"Thank you." Normally, I'd have to overhead page for

30

a stocker and we'd all stand here staring at one another while we waited for someone to bring a fresh carton. But I never have to do that when Tyson is my bagger. He always runs for me.

He truly is the nicest boy in the universe.

I must be actually smiling—not just in my head—because my customer gives me a wary look. Like maybe she thinks I'm nuts. I resist the urge to sing along with "Jingle Bells."

Tyson comes back just about the time I start to feel nervous laughter bubble up in my chest. I've already finished swiping everything else from the customer's cart, and bagged what was still in reach.

"Here you go, ma'am." He presents her with a fresh carton of eggs, already opened for her inspection. He can totally get away with calling women "ma'am." Even young ones. I think it's because of that slight Southern accent.

The customer's expression softens. "Thank you," she says. I snap the lid to scan the code and finally finish this transaction.

"Guess who's here," Tyson says after the customer has pushed her loaded cart away.

"Who?"

"Coupon Lady."

Coupon Lady is one of those extreme couponers who

carries a binder full of clippings, only buys things on sale, and usually ends up walking away from the store with hundreds of dollars' worth of groceries for, like, $3.79. It's impressive, but getting her at your register is about the worst thing that can happen to a cashier. It can literally mean hours with her staring at your screen to make sure every cent is accounted for. I got her during my second week on the job and almost broke down in tears before it was over.

"On Christmas Eve?" Not even crazy Coupon Lady could be this crazy, could she?

"Crap, how far is she through the store?" Sammi, who is bagging for Zaina, demands. I didn't realize she was paying attention to us.

"She was in Dairy," Tyson says.

"Who?" Zaina speaks up for the first time in ages.

"Coupon Lady," I answer, scanning my next customer's cereal without looking. Only the double beep from the register alerts me that something is wrong. I refocus and have to take an extra item off the total. My customer sighs.

"Why is she here today?" Zaina whispers.

"She'll go for the shortest line. Try to look busier," Sammi instructs Zaina.

"How am I supposed to do that?"

"I don't know. Just do it!"

Tyson laughs. "What do you want her to do, run in place?"

"Anything to make our line longer." Sammi puts a few items into the reusable bag open in front of her. "Free cookies to the next twenty customers in lane five!" she suddenly shouts.

A few people look over with interest.

"Free cookies?" someone asks.

"Sure! Why not?"

"You don't even have any cookies," Tyson says.

"I will find some cookies if it means I can avoid bagging groceries for Coupon Lady. I'll take 'em from the Break Room."

"You're going to steal our Christmas cookies?" he asks.

"Whatever it takes, man."

"Who's stealing Christmas cookies?" Kris cuts into our conversation, arriving suddenly from behind Tyson.

"Sammi's trying to avoid Coupon Lady," Tyson says.

"Oh." Kris leans back as understanding dawns. He focuses on Sammi. "By stealing cookies?" Before she can answer, he shakes his head. "Never mind. Nobody's taking the cookies. I need somebody to go for carts."

Sammi's hand shoots in the air. "I volunteer as tribute!"

I laugh. Loud. Loud enough to startle a few customers and make me slap my hand over my mouth.

Kris cocks an eyebrow at me, but responds to Sammi. "You know it started snowing out there?"

"Don't care."

"More like sleeting."

"Don't care." Sammi unties her apron and thrusts it at Kris. "I'll be back."

My hands, which are still blindly passing groceries over the scanner, bump into the plastic divider at the end of the order. I look up into the annoyed face of a customer.

"Hi there! Did you find everything you were looking for today?"

"Yeah." She sticks out her hand, a credit card tweezed between two fingers.

Red-faced, I hit the total button, already trying to jam the card through the reader.

"Chloe." Kris calls from the end of the lane. "Break time."

"Now?" This is earlier than I expected, but at least I won't get Coupon Lady.

"Yeah. Now." He keys the mic on his walkie-talkie. "Gabe, I need you on lane six. ASAP." There's a crackly response from Gabe, and Kris points at me. "When he gets here, take your ten minutes, okay?" He's gone before I can even respond.

"I've never seen Kris this stressed out," I say.

"I don't think I've ever seen him work this hard," Tyson says with a grin.

While I wait for Gabe, I start on the next customer. It's one of our regulars, though when I greet her she doesn't seem to recognize me. Very self-esteem building, this job.

Gabe squeezes past the cart at Zaina's register and invades my tiny square of personal space. "Greetings," he announces. "Now get out."

"Real nice, Gabe." I frown at him, flicking my eyes toward my customer. This regular is not exactly renowned for her forgiving nature.

Gabe turns on the charm like a switch. "Mrs. Hudson, I didn't see you there!" he says. "Happy holidays!"

Mrs. Hudson smiles for the first time since I laid eyes on her. "Gabe!" she says. "I didn't know you were on today."

Gabe sighs and shakes his head. "Sadly, I'm just the backup this morning, but as luck would have it, I'm here to relieve Chloe right this very instant."

"That is lucky," she says. Mrs. Hudson has to be in her mid-to-late forties. I've never seen her in anything but high-end workout clothes, and her purchases are as predictable as her yoga pants: fresh fruit, Vitamin Water, this organic brand of cereal that looks from the picture like it might actually be made from wood chips and seeds, and fat-free yogurt.

Even on Christmas Eve. Ho ho ho!

Overhead, the PA fades out "Rudolph the Red-Nosed Reindeer" and transitions into "Holly Jolly Christmas." I cringe. This one might have to go on my least-favorites list.

"Go 'head, Chloe," Gabe says, nudging me with his shoulder.

"Let me just—" I start to protest. We're supposed to always finish with the current customer and log out of the register when we go on break.

"I'll log you out. Just go."

I give him a look.

"Seriously, I got this. Take your break. I've got a bunch of other people to relieve after you. Go."

Holding my hands up in resignation, I squeeze past the cart to my right, trying my hardest not to dislodge the little boy standing on the end with his arms hanging over the basket. The cart bumps into the sidewall, though, and he sticks his tongue out at me. It's hard not to do the same back at him, but instead, I smile. Little does he know it's my "go jump in a lake" smile.

Still I don't leave. I'm watching Gabe to make sure he

logs me out when he finishes with Mrs. Hudson.

Kris walks by with his walkie-talkie in hand. "Chloe, you *can* leave the floor when you're on break. That's kind of the point." He winks at me. "Tyson, I need you to go out and do carts."

"But Sammi just went."

"Apparently, it's bad out there. Can you please go help her?"

"What about—?" Tyson points at the long line of people still waiting for Gabe to check them out.

"Gabe's going to have to check and bag," Kris says, already moving on to his next thing. I feel bad for him. This is definitely not his kind of day.

Tyson waits until Kris is out of earshot, then looks at me. "You and I both know that Gabe cannot check and bag."

This is true.

THINGS GABE ROSSI IS GOOD AT
1. Being charming.
2. Flirting with the middle-aged yoga moms.
3. Playing basketball—according to him.
4. Getting the credit-card scanner to work even when no one else can seem to make it read.

THINGS GABE ROSSI IS NOT GOOD AT
1. Getting to work on time.
2. Bagging groceries.
3. Working the register and bagging groceries at the same time.
4. Not flirting with middle-aged yoga moms.


"Maybe carts can wait until I get back from my break," I suggest. "I can check and bag while you go out."

"Maybe." Tyson steps back to squint toward the front of the store, where the carts are stored. Or, where they would be stored, if there were any. "It doesn't look good."

"I'll bag for you." I'm already reaching for the next item to come down the conveyor. Incidentally, Mrs. Hudson's Vitamin Water.

"Kris might get mad if you stay on the floor."

"Then I'll go get carts," I decide.

Tyson looks at me from the corner of his eye. "No offense, but, you?"

"Hey, I could do it!" I strike a body-builder pose, realizing too late it's going to make me look even geekier than usual.

Tyson chuckles, tipping his head down to look at me over the rims of his glasses.

"It would be more impressive if I didn't have this

thermal on." I pluck at the sleeve of the gray thermal shirt I put on under my red holiday GoodFoods T-shirt. It's too cold to spend the day in short sleeves.

"It would be more impressive if there was anything under that thermal," Tyson teases, squeezing my nonexistent bicep.

I bite my lip, startled by the contact. *Please don't blush, please don't blush,* I beg my body.

Tyson pulls his hand back and drums it against his leg. "You should go before Kris comes back."

"I'm getting carts," I tell him.

"Don't worry. I'll take care of it."

"No. I'll do it." Just because I've never gotten carts before doesn't mean I can't do it, right? How hard can it be?

I code my way into the Break Room and get my coat and gloves from my locker, knocking my lunch bag to the floor in the process. I'm supposed to have a snack during my break, but I'm determined to help Tyson. So I reach blindly into the bag and come out with a stick of string cheese. Good old Mom. I can get it down with two bites. It should hold me for a while.

My apron sticks out from beneath my jacket when I zip it up, making me feel stupid for not taking it off. None of the people who regularly go out for carts have their aprons poking out beneath their jackets. Oh well.

Outside, the weather hits me like a brick wall. Kris wasn't kidding. There is *something* falling from the sky, but it can't seem to decide if it's rain or snow. My shoes squelch in the dark-gray slop splattered all over the blacktop.

I spot Sammi working at one of the cart corrals. She has the little red machine that powers all the carts in a long train back to the building. I dart around a few cars cruising for spots and call out to her.

"I'm here to help!"

"You?" she asks. "Why did Kris send you?"

"He didn't. I'm supposed to be on break. But it's crazy in there. No one else can come."

"Wouldn't you rather go on break?"

"I don't mind." I really don't. I always feel singularly useless on my required breaks. They never come at a time when I could actually use one. I'd rather just work straight through and get the day over with.

Sammi braces her foot against a particularly stubborn pair of carts and wrestles one free. "Was Tyson supposed to come out?"

My ears get hot, and a trickle of melting sleet drizzles down my neck. I hope the cold covers up my involuntary blushing. "Yeah, but he's gotta bag for Gabe."

Sammi snorts. "No kidding. Gabe needs all the help he can get."

"So, what should I do?"

She arches one dark eyebrow until it nearly disappears under her platinum swoop of bangs, now matted to her forehead with precipitation. "I usually go with: get the carts."

"Okay." *No need to get nasty,* I think. I should say it, but I've never been one for confrontation. Even less so since we moved and I lost Eva. Although not making waves hasn't been all that effective as a friend-making strategy, if I think about it.

Leaving Sammi at the crowded cart corral, I decide to try the next one down the same parking row. It's farther out, and has fewer carts in it. Probably a good place to start for my first time.

There are huge, sloppy puddles of slush around the corral, and icy water oozes through the eyelets at the bottom of my Converse All-Stars. But that's barely noticeable compared to how badly my nose is running. This is not a glamorous job, and I'm not sorry I've never done it before.

I get a short train of carts going. It's not bad at first, but once there are four of them linked, the weight becomes a serious force to be reckoned with. By the time

I've gathered all seven, I can't move them.

"Sammi!" I shout. There's no way I'll get these back to her on my own. "Sammi!"

She doesn't hear me.

I don't want to walk away from my effort, especially since the linked carts are partially blocking the neighboring car.

"Sammi!" I try again.

No response.

All right. I have to figure this out. Stepping back a few feet, I gather myself with a quick breath, then take a running start. My hands hit the plastic handle of the last cart, jarring my arms up through my elbows, but the train moves! I let out a triumphant "Ha!" and drive my feet into the pavement, leaning into the inertia of the carts with everything I've got.

Now that they're in motion, it's a little easier. I get them past two cars before the trouble starts.

I've been staring at the ground, head bent into the effort, and when I look up, I see that the lead cart is no longer directly in front of me. It's taken a distinct right turn, like a drunk leading a conga line. In fact, it's headed straight for a parked car, with the weight of the six carts behind it joining in the effort.

"No!" I shout, pulling up to an abrupt stop. All I succeed in doing, though, is loosening the last cart from the line. I try to run ahead and grab the leader, but I'm too late.

With a sickening crunch, the carts ram into the bumper of a silver Toyota.

My hands fly up to my mouth. Footsteps come toward me and suddenly Sammi is there, yanking on the carts.

"What did you do?" she hisses.

"I'm sorry! I didn't—"

"Jesus, Chloe! Look at this!"

The corner of the bumper is cracked, as though a giant child has picked it up and casually tapped it on the ground.

"Oh my God!" Tears sting the back of my eyes.

"Come on! Get it together." Sammi gives the train of carts another huge tug and suddenly they're back on a straight path. She looks around the lot quickly. "Go to the back. Push!"

"What?"

"Push!" she shouts.

"But—"

"Damn, Chloe, would you just frigging push?!"

I scurry back, still sniffling, and once again hurl myself at the carts to get them rolling. Sammi pulls on the lead cart until we have all seven past the train she already constructed. Together we muscle the carts into line, getting them connected to the front of the red Mule.

She has me hold the last one in place while she stretches out a long bungee cord to lash them all together.

"Now we go inside," she says.

"What about the car?"

"Look." Her gloved finger extends to the large white sign presiding over the cart corral. Under the friendly, green letters that spell out *Please return your carts here!* are smaller, more businesslike black letters that read, *GoodFoods Market is not responsible for damage caused to vehicles by shopping carts.*

"Don't worry about it," Sammi says.

"But it's my fault. I *am* responsible."

She rolls her eyes and flips the switch on the Mule's remote to start the long train moving toward the store's entrance. I hurry to keep up as she walks alongside the front of the train, occasionally pushing or pulling on one of the carts to redirect the line.

"Shouldn't I at least tell Kris?" I ask.

"No, you definitely shouldn't," she responds. "There are big signs all over the parking lot that say we're not responsible for anything that happens out here."

"That just means if other people damage their cars, we can't do anything about it."

"You weren't even supposed to be here. So, guess who's going to get blamed?" She glares at me and jerks her thumb toward her chest. "Me. I was on cart duty. And you'll probably get your precious little boyfriend, Tyson, in trouble, too. Is that what you want?"

"No!" I shake my head hard enough to make my glasses slide down my nose. "And he's not my boyfriend."

"Whatever. Do yourself a favor and forget about it." She guides the carts through the small opening at the front of the store. The onslaught of wintery rain/snow lessens now that we're near the building.

I swipe at my forehead to stop more water from drizzling behind my glasses. "What if whoever owns the car reports the damage?"

"Then Kris'll tell them the same thing he tells everybody: 'we are not responsible for any damage to cars in the parking lot.'"

"What about the security cameras?"

Sammi shrugs. "There are two, and they only cover about a third of the lot. There's a big blind spot where we were. Nobody saw anything. You'll be fine. Just keep your mouth shut." She pulls the Mule free of the cart conga line and starts steering it toward the entrance.

My stomach rolls. "I don't know about this."

She cocks her head at me. "If you're going to freak out, they're definitely going to know you did it. Are you going to freak out?"

I consider the question. It certainly feels like I could freak out. In fact, I might already be freaking out. I'm afraid to speak, so I just nod.

Sighing, Sammi says, "Stay here." She guides the Mule back into the store and a few seconds later she's back, grabbing me by the elbow and heading out into the sloppy parking lot once more.

"What are we doing?" I ask. We're in the aisle where the damaged car is parked. I wonder if we're going to take down the license number, or maybe leave a note. The idea both terrifies and relieves me.

"We're going for cigarettes."

"What?"

She digs in her coat pocket and comes up with a small orange box. "I'm almost out. I need smokes; you need a break."

"But I'm already on break. . . ."

"Not that kind of break. Come on."

I don't even realize where we're headed until we're almost at the small line of bare shrubs between the parking lot and the sidewalk.

"We're not supposed to leave on break," I say.

"Good thing we're not on break, then," Sammi says, and steps between two of the knee-high bushes. She's still holding my elbow, so I don't have much of a choice but to follow her.

"Where are we going?"

"Just across the street." She pauses at the curb to let a herd of cars rush by. The tires kick up slush, spattering our jeans from the knees down, but it hardly matters given how soaked we already are.

There's a break in the traffic, and Sammi darts into the road. I don't realize she's let go of my arm until I find myself running after her. I have no idea why I'm going along on this errand. Sammi and I aren't exactly friends.

## THINGS I HAVE LEARNED ABOUT SAMMI (FROM A SERIOUS DISTANCE)

1. She must get her hair cut all the time, because she wears a kind of pixie cut with a long sweep of bangs, and her hair never gets long enough to cover her ears.

2. She laughs a lot, but always in these sharp *hehs* that remind me of a car that won't start.

3. The only person I see her talk to regularly at work is Gabe,

which is weird because I can't figure out what they could possibly have in common.

4. The first time I met her, I thought she was a boy until she started talking.

5. She scares me a little. It has nothing to do with mistaking her for a boy. There's just something about her. Like maybe she can't stand me.

Yet here we are, jogging across the tarmac of a gas station to the convenience store. Sammi pushes the door open and we walk inside. She takes a deep breath and exhales with a grin. "Don't you love the smell of overcooked hot dogs in the morning?"

I look at her, trying to decide if she's joking. I think she is. "I prefer congealed nacho-cheese scent, myself."

She lets out one of those trademark *heh!* laughs and heads for the front of the store. The clerk finishes with his current customer, then whirls around to silence an alarm coming from a display behind him. The gesture looks practiced and unconcerned. I squint at the display, and realize it's the control panel for the gas pumps. I hope that wasn't the bad kind of alarm.

"Any gas?" he asks Sammi when she leans on the counter.

"Nope. American Spirit, organic mellow," she says. "It's the orange pack."

"I know which pack it is," he snaps, reaching up to the hidden rack of cigarettes over the glass partition.

My body tenses, waiting for him to card her. I don't think Sammi is eighteen yet, though that's just another factoid I could add to a long list of things I don't know about her.

Sammi digs a small collection of wadded bills out of her pocket. The clerk gives us the eye as he straightens out the bills, but the money's all there and he never asks for ID.

"You need anything?" she asks me, tipping her head toward the counter.

"I don't smoke," I say.

One of her dark eyebrows lifts. "They *do* sell other things, you know."

"I'm fine," I say.

"Done freaking out?"

"Um . . ." This is a good question. At the moment, I'm so distracted by leaving work without notice and standing around all awkward while Sammi buys cigarettes illegally, that I've kind of forgotten about the cart incident. Which I suppose was her point.

Suddenly, Sammi's already-pale face goes a shade

49

whiter and her permasmirk drops. "Oh shit!" she whispers, looking over my shoulder.

"What?"

Without explaining, she grabs a fistful of my coat and drags me away from the counter. I stumble behind her past the rolling hot-dog cooker, the congealing vat of nacho cheese, and the soda machine. She hauls me all the way to the end of the first aisle and around the corner, then drops to a crouch between a display of motor oil and the cold-drink cases. I nearly fall on top of her, and gasp when my knee smacks the ground.

"Sammi! What the hell?"

"Shh!" She gives me a stern look and whips her hand up to make the shushing gesture. "Kris is here," she says in a voice so quiet, it's barely more than a breath with shape.

My eyes nearly fall out of my head. Does he know about the car in the parking lot? Oh God, I'm going to be arrested on Christmas Eve!

Sammi's got her head tilted up and I follow her gaze to find one of those huge convex mirrors that shows the clerk a warped view of the entire store. Near the register, I can make out a person with dark hair, like Kris, but I can't be sure that it's him with the fun-house effect of the mirror. At the bottom of the curve, there are two humanish blobs.

The only clue as to who we are is Sammi's platinum-blond hair. It's like a beacon of light against the dark display of car products behind us. My own hair—normally a stand-out being red—is so darkened by the slushy rain that it looks more brown in the reflection. Sammi must be thinking the same thing, because she gropes at her coat until she gets the hood up and over her hair.

"What's he doing here?" I whisper.

"How should I know?"

I watch his every move, certain he's going to march straight down the aisle to grab us and drag us back to work. Or possibly to jail. It's so hot in the store, and the smell of overcooked microwave burrito is intense back here. Sweat prickles in my armpits, and I want to unzip my coat, but I don't dare move.

Sammi's mouth is moving. I realize she's murmuring, "Don't look at me, don't look at me," which is oddly something of a relief. I would have pictured her being cool and calm. But she's as nervous as I am.

Of course, at that moment, the alarm on my watch goes off. It's my snack reminder. The tiny electronic beeps sound like the wailing alarm in a prison-escape movie to my ears. I expect searchlights to scan the convenience store for us.

I scramble with my coat sleeve to get my wrist free and squeeze all the buttons on the watch at once, trying to shut it off.

"Jesus Christ, Chloe," Sammi hisses.

"I'm sorry!"

We both check the mirror to see Kris on the move. I suck in a breath and prepare myself for capture. But he just heads for the door, setting off a soft *bong, bong* chime somewhere in the store as he goes out into the wet weather once more.

Relief makes me crumple over, hands on my knees.

"Oh my God, that was close." I sigh.

Sammi barks out a couple short laughs. "Oh, man."

"What are you doing back there, girlies?" the clerk shouts, craning to see us in the mirror. "No shoplifting! I'll call the police!"

"I already bought something, remember?" Sammi says, standing up and waggling her pack of American Spirits in the air. "I'm a paying customer!"

"You buy something else, or you go," he declares.

"Jeez, what a dick," she mutters.

"Go now," the clerk says, pointing at the door.

She opens her mouth, but I cut her off.

"We're going." This time it's my turn to take Sammi

by the elbow and lead the way outside.

My nerves can't take any more of this. I have to get back to GoodFoods and find out if the owner of the car I hit is going to send me to jail for the rest of my life. Or call my mother.

I'm not sure which would be worse.

TOP TEN THINGS MY MOTHER CAN NEVER EVER FIND
OUT ABOUT

10. That it was me who broke the crystal champagne flutes.

9. That David used to let me drive before I had my license.

8. That I wasn't sick on the day of tryouts for the marching
band—I just didn't want to be in the band again.

7. That Eva's mom used to buy us tickets to R-rated movies
when I said we were going to PG-13 ones.

6. That I really hate her sugar-free cookies.

5. That Eva hasn't called me in two months, so I don't think
we're friends anymore.

4. That sometimes when I tell her I'm meeting some people from
school, I just go to a coffee shop and read my book for a
few hours so she doesn't think I'm a friendless loser.

3. That our old neighbors' nephew once offered me five dollars if

I'd show him my boobs, and I might have done it if his mom hadn't come into the backyard then.

2. That I got pulled over for speeding and claimed my insulin pump was running low to get out of the ticket.

1. That I crashed a bunch of carts into a parked car at work and didn't tell anyone.

Before we even reach the road, I notice the news van. It's from one of the local stations, and it's parked in the fire lane at the front of the store.

My first thought, of course, is that the customer whose car I hit called Action12 to come down here and kick some butt. On further reflection, it seems unlikely that would be anyone's first step.

"What do you think that's about?" Sammi asks.

"Not sure." But in my head I'm already composing a list.

POSSIBLE EXPLANATIONS FOR THE LOCAL NEWS AT GOODFOODS

1. One of those lame stories about the retail rush before Christmas.

2. A lottery winner bought their ticket at this store.

3. We've been reported to Action12 for some kind of health violation.

4. There's been a major recall on something, like chicken, beef, or baby formula.
5. The president of the United States dropped by for some eggnog.


I admit some are likelier than others.

I lead Sammi back down the aisle where I hit the car, and to my immense relief, the car's gone.

Gone!

It would still be here if the owner had gone back in to report the damage, right? Am I seriously in the clear?

"Look." I nudge Sammi. "The car's not here anymore."

"Told you it was no big deal."

"I still feel bad about it."

"Obviously they don't," she says.

"I guess."

"No point in freaking out, anyway. It's not like you wrote down the license-plate number. You can't do anything about it now."

She's right. But I do remember the numbers and the first two letters. I think.

Inside the store, Sammi and I take a moment to shake the excess water from our coats and blot our faces before stepping off the black industrial mats the store puts down in the winter.

"Thanks, Sammi," I say.

She rolls her eyes. "Whatever. Just as long as you're not going to get me in trouble."

Hopefully, that translates to *You're welcome.*

We pass through the second set of doors and right away it's clear where the news crew is. There is a crowd gathered near Customer Service, with a boom mic extended over everyone's heads. There's also a big camera with a bright light attached to the top.

"What the hell?" Sammi wonders.

"I don't know."

The entrance to the Break Room is right behind the Customer Service desk, so we have to approach the mob. Nothing like the possibility of being on camera to make you self-conscious. I pat the top of my head, thinking I'll smooth my wind-frazzled hair, but it's so wet there's no point. Great. With any luck they'll want to interview me and I'll be captured for all eternity looking like I just got pulled out of a river.

As I'm reaching for the door, Kris opens it and we all jump back in surprise. He catches the door before it closes again.

"What happened to you?" he asks me.

"I went outside for a few minutes." That's true, anyway.

"What's all that about?" Sammi asks, jerking her thumb in the direction of Customer Service.

"It's that charity thing, I think." He rubs his temple distractedly.

Oh yeah. You'd think I could have put that together considering the fluorescent-green Christmas Eve memos tacked up all over the Break Room.

"Are we supposed to do anything?" I ask.

"Smile, smile, smile!" he says with a big, cheesy one of his own.

Sammi grits her teeth. "Smiling's my favorite!"

Kris laughs, a much more typical expression of easy humor sliding over his face for a second. "Well, then today's your lucky day!"

Sammi rolls her eyes again and I follow her into the Break Room, already working my coat off. I have to get my register back from Gabe before he does something irreparable to my totals.

Sammi doesn't say anything to me as she stashes her coat in her locker and heads back to the floor. Just when I thought I might have broken the ice.

At least I learned one thing about her—she smokes

some weird brand of cigarettes I've never heard of. That's one down, two to go for my first goal for the day. And so far, I haven't written down any lists. I'm doing pretty well.

Back out in the store, the district manager, Mr. Solomon, is in front of the cameras with some people I don't recognize. They're talking and laughing in that fake way people do when they're humoring someone.

By my calculation, about thirty percent of adulthood is pretending to like people you actually couldn't care less about.

"Hey!" Tyson says as I move up the lane to take my place at register six. "You all right?"

"Carts are in." Never mind the state of the cars in the parking lot.

His face lights up. "Thank you! You're a lifesaver."

I shake my head. "Don't worry about it." And don't thank me. I could have gotten all of us in trouble.

Gabe relinquishes my register and moves over one to give Zaina her break. I try to smile at her, but she's watching the crowd near Customer Service.

A woman wearing a fleece vest and cargo pants with a headset and a clipboard is moving along the ends of the registers. When she reaches Zaina's lane, she marches up to the register with her hand already stuck out for shaking.

"Hi! I'm Connie. I'm a producer for WACJ. We're going to put a few employees in the shot for when Gene opens the box. We'd like you to be one of those people."

"Me?" Zaina looks confused.

"Uh-huh!" Connie puts her hand on Zaina's back and gives her a little shove toward the crowd.

Of course they'd pick her. Who wouldn't want the beautiful girl in the picture? I push my glasses up my nose and feel the squelching in my wet shoes as I shift my feet. I am so not going to get picked.

"You too, okay?" Connie says in her syrupy voice to Tyson.

"Me?" he echoes Zaina's response.

"Uh-huh!" she chirps again.

Tyson looks at me. "You okay to bag for yourself?"

I nod. "You bet. Go ahead." Which, if he were psychic, he would know meant, *Kiss me.*

I get through two customers before the commotion at the Customer Service desk pulls my attention again. It's pulled everyone's attention, I realize, looking down the row of registers. Now that some people have moved out of the way for the camera, I can see exactly what the producer was up to. She "randomly" picked Zaina, who is Middle Eastern (maybe); Tyson, who is black; Agnes, who is older than dirt; a stocker named Miguel, who is Mexican; an older checker named Tasha, who is also black; and a woman from Bakery, who is one of those all-American types with blond hair and blue eyes. I feel like I'm looking at a college brochure: *Look how diverse our student population is! Look, here are some brown people lounging in the quad together!* It's embarrassing.

I wonder how the "randomly" chosen feel about this. Is that the sort of thing I can ask Tyson? It's so hard to tell what's a good conversation starter and what's my inability to stop babbling.

The producer also seems to be keeping the more color-fully dressed customers out of the shot. It's Christmas Eve, so of course there are people in Santa hats, ugly Christmas sweaters—some ironic, some definitely not ironic—and light-up jewelry, but they're really nothing compared to what people normally wear.

People seem to think they're invisible in the grocery store. Like it's just an oversized extension of their houses. I'm not sure why. I mean, they have to get in the car and drive here, don't they? They should be fully aware they're going out in public. But based on months of observation, it seems clear to me that the vast majority of people really have no clue.

# TOP TEN WEIRDEST CLOTHING ITEMS SEEN ON GOODFOODS CUSTOMERS

10. Pajamas. And not just pajama pants and a T-shirt. I'm talking nightgowns, slippers, and/or robes.

9. Boxer shorts. This one seems to be perpetrated only by high-school girls, but I've definitely seen it.

8. Offensive T-shirts. I'm all for freedom of speech, so I'm not talking about shirts that might be controversial. I'm talking about plain disgusting things, like *Show me your boobs*. That's not even an opinion. It's just gross.

7. Costumes. This is probably my favorite on the list. Mostly occurs at Halloween, but can happen anytime. It's not just kids, either. You haven't lived until you've seen a grown man dressed as a nun buying a case of beer.

6. Inappropriate hats. Not offensive hats, but hats that don't seem to "go" with the rest of a person's outfit. For example, a man in a tracksuit and a cowboy hat.

5. Hip-waders. Meaning the rubber overalls that fishermen wear to stand in a river. I can't imagine what that guy thought he was going to encounter in the store that would require hip-waders, but there he was. Ironically, he bought frozen fish sticks.

4. Workout clothes. I get that it's pretty much acceptable to wear your gym gear out in the world, but most of the time, people cover up a little bit. I sold a bottle of water and a pack of

gum to a woman in a sports bra and tiny bike shorts a few months ago. It was about thirty-five degrees outside.

3. A hospital gown. Actually, this was one of the most understandable incidents, because the guy had been in a car accident and was stopping at the store on the way home from the hospital to get his prescription filled at the store pharmacy. He told me his shirt got ruined and this was all they had for him to wear. At least he had pants on.

2. Obvious undergarments. I thought the trend of letting your thong show out the top of your pants was over until I started working at GoodFoods. The worst offender was an obviously male patron—he had a beard, an Adam's apple, and a deep baritone voice—wearing a bra. I saw it right though his T-shirt. It was dark, maybe purple or navy blue, and I could even see the little bow in the middle. There is no reasonable explanation.

1. No underwear. I haven't been subjected to this awfulness since it got cold out, but over the summer there was more than one incident where women came in wearing a short dress—short enough to be a shirt, really—and managed to give me a flash of their—ahem—assets while unloading their carts. Were these swimsuit cover-ups and they just didn't want to leave wet butt prints on the upholstery in their cars? I hoped so, but then why stop and do a week's worth of grocery shopping?

People are truly weird.

Connie, the industrious producer, has managed to usher the man in the Birkenstocks, black socks, and bare legs poking out of his parka to the side, along with a woman wearing a lacy bustier and a fur-trimmed miniskirt.

Mr. Solomon begins his speech. "We are so proud to once again be partnering with Full Hearts Full Plates to bring holiday meals to local families in need. Last year, GoodFoods raised over thirty thousand dollars for Full Hearts Full Plates, and I can tell you we are already on track to blow that number out of the water!" There is a smattering of applause, which the chosen employees join a little late. Their expressions range from rapturous (Agnes) to nervous (Zaina).

Mr. Solomon continues. "The generosity of our customers is unparalleled. It's due to all of you"—he extends his arms to indicate all of the customers queued up at the registers—"that we are able to help those in need in our community.

"And now, without further ado, let's get this year's total added up!" He turns slightly, drawing my eye to the big wooden box that's been sitting on the Customer Service counter since the day after Halloween.

It's meticulously wrapped in pale-blue wrapping paper decorated with glittering white snowflakes. Even the inside of the slit in the top is covered. When Mr. Solomon spins it around, I notice that the panel in the back that opens the box is wrapped separately. This kind of attention to detail has Agnes written all over it.

Mr. Solomon produces a key and opens the padlock holding the panel shut. He chuckles softly. "I feel like Santa Claus!"

Personally, I don't see how, but there is polite laughter from other people.

He eases the panel down as if expecting an avalanche of cash to bust out, cartoon-style. But after peeking inside, he lets the panel drop wide open.

Even from my station at the register I can see that the box is essentially empty.

Mr. Solomon laughs nervously, and reaches inside. He comes back with a few bills in his hand, but that's it. Wide-eyed, he looks at the reporter standing to his right, who is smiling and gazing into the camera as if nothing is wrong. Next, he tries the producer. "Can we stop?"

"Cut!" she says, stepping in front of the camera.

Suddenly everyone is crowding toward Mr. Solomon and the randomly selected employees, who look completely confused and helpless.

"What's going on?" I wonder to Gabe, still standing at Zaina's register.

Gabe laughs. "Guess our customers aren't as generous as he thought."

"What are we supposed to do?"

"Nothing," he says. "What would we do about it?"

Mr. Solomon's voice booms over the murmurs of the crowd. "Ladies and gentlemen, thank you for your attention. We're going to add up our total now and then we'll be ready to present the check to Full Hearts Full Plates." It's a normal-enough-sounding statement, but there is something off with his tone of voice.

"This is hilarious," Sammi says. She's back at the bagging station at the end of Gabe's register, grinning like the Cheshire cat.

Tyson emerges from the crowd and shrugs when he sees me looking.

"What's happening?" Sammi asks him as he takes up his station at the end of my lane.

"Don't know," he says. "I guess there was supposed to be a lot more money in there."

Sammi cackles. "How much was there?"

"It looked like maybe twenty or thirty bucks."

"How much was he expecting?" I wonder.

"More than that, I guess."

"Our customers are total tightwads." Sammi grins that catlike smile again.

Zaina drifts by to take her register back. "There is money missing," she says.

"Is that what they said?" Tyson asks.

"No. But I know there is money missing." She pauses between Sammi and Tyson. "My mother gives me money to put in the box each time I work. It's not there."

## PROGRESS ON TODAY'S TO-DO LIST

1. Talk to at least three of my coworkers long enough to learn something new about them. CHECK. So far I've learned that Sammi smokes American Spirit, Zaina donates money every time she works, and Tyson calls his aunts his *aunties* (which is completely swoon-worthy, obviously).

2. Try not to let my mouth take over my brain during those conversations. CHECK(ish). At least I haven't totally humiliated myself.

3. Actually remember to turn off my ringer when I get to work. FAIL, but I'm totally doing it right now, and no one called me so it didn't ring in my pocket—ha!

4. Make no more than three lists during the day. CHECK. (But only if I don't count the ones I've made in my head.)

5. Pick up the Christmas ham Mom ordered from the butcher

department. FAIL. I absolutely have to remember this or my mother will disown me.

6. Give Tyson a ride home. FAIL! I haven't even offered yet! I am so weak!

I used to hate the song "All I Want for Christmas Is You." I don't know why exactly, but it was the sort of song that made me sigh when I heard it in a store or on the radio in the car. And at Christmas, you hear it a lot. Now I kind of love it.

Why the change of heart? It's all because Tyson finds it irresistible. I don't know if he's aware that he does it, but it's the song most likely to make him get into a full groove. He does a fair amount of swaying and nodding with the beat, humming under his breath for a lot of songs. But "All I Want for Christmas Is You" comes on, and he's just a few degrees short of putting on a show at the end of lane six.

He's dancing right now, and it's killing me that I have to keep my back turned to him to finish totaling up my customer's order. When I finally turn to see him again, he's got one of our little-old-lady regular customers by the hand, and he's dancing her in a circle while she laughs and pink spots rise in her cheeks.

I have never wanted to be a little old lady so much in my life.

From two lanes over, one of the other baggers pitches a wad of paper at the back of his head. Tyson ignores the assault and leads the regular under his arm in a slow turn. Her wrinkled face is beaming when she turns back and pats him on the chest.

"You *are* a charmer," she says.

I sigh and resist the urge to prop both elbows on the conveyor belt to watch him without my pesky job interrupting. He *is* a charmer. But not in the same way that Gabe is. It's like Tyson isn't even aware of it. He can't help himself.

"Where did you learn to dance?" I ask.

"Who learns to dance?" He shrugs. "I just dance."

"Do you only dance with little old ladies, or do you give girls your own age a chance?" I can hardly believe it when the words come out of my mouth. I thought it would sound kind of funny, but instead I sound like I am blatantly flirting.

Great.

And now I'm blushing.

"I can dance with *anybody*," he says.

My heart stutters in my chest, and my mouth goes too dry to say anything.

A customer saves me from potential humiliation by asking, "Young lady, are you open?"

"Yes!" I nearly shout. "Come on down! How are you today? Did you find everything you were looking for? Thank you for choosing GoodFoods!" I'm still talking too loud. And out of order. God. What is wrong with me?

Behind me, Tyson chuckles, and goes back to singing softly along with Mariah Carey.

I concentrate on my job for a few customers. Better not risk more embarrassing behavior too soon. And now I'm afraid to make the usual chitchat, because I'm convinced I'll be all loud and unintelligible.

If I had a free second, I'd write a list to get my brain back in order. For now, I'm stuck thinking of one in my head.

WHAT I KNOW FOR SURE ABOUT THE MISSING MONEY

1. Zaina's mom gives her money to put into the box every time she works.

2. She told us it's always a twenty-dollar bill.

3. From their angle, Zaina and Tyson agree there was only one twenty-dollar bill in the handful that Mr. Solomon pulled out.

4. It's possible that there were a few more bills in the bottom of the box, but definitely not enough to make up for the number Zaina must have put in.

5. The lock didn't appear to be broken when Mr. Solomon used the key, but no one saw it up close.
6. Mr. Solomon and the box disappeared into the Count Out room right after he made his announcement.

On paper—or in my head, in this case—it's a bit of a mystery. Not exactly something you'd alert the FBI over, but at least it's something to keep my brain occupied.

I'm in the middle of changing my register tape when Sammi rushes by in lane five. Zaina's gone on lunch so her register is closed, and it's the only open path from the main store to the front area. Sammi's got a weird look on her face and I can't help following her with my eyes as she runs to the ladies' room.

Jogging a few steps behind her is Gabe. He stops near me when he sees her disappear into the bathroom.

"Shit," he breathes.

"What's wrong?" I ask.

"Sammi cut herself back in Dairy."

"I think I might have a bandage in my drawer." There are often a few under the tills in the registers because we tend to get a lot of paper cuts opening bags and dealing with the register tape.

"It's pretty bad." Gabe makes a face. "Shit." The word is barely audible.

"What happened?" Tyson asks.

"I don't know." He shoves his brown hair back with one hand. "We were stocking dip, and she had the box cutter. I tried to help, but it's bad."

"She wouldn't let you?" I guess.

"I wasn't thinking, I just—" He shakes his head as if coming out of trance. "Forget it. She's gone now." One hand on his hip, he makes a helpless gesture toward the ladies' room.

"Do you want me to check on her?" I ask.

He thinks about it. "Someone should."

"Okay."

I let him take over my register again and head for the bathroom. Once I reach the door, I hesitate. Sammi and I may have bonded a little over the cart incident this morning, but I'm not sure I'm the person she'll want to see right now.

I push the door open slightly. "Sammi?"

"Who is it?" she asks.

"Chloe. Novak." Why did I say that?

"What do you want?"

"Gabe said you cut yourself." I push the door open farther and step in. "Do you need help?"

Even as I'm asking, I can see that she does. She's at one of the sinks with her left thumb clenched in her opposite hand. There's blood oozing between her fingers.

"What happened?"

"Stupid box cutter!" she hisses.

"Is it bad?" I approach the sink, reaching hesitantly for her hand. "Gabe said it was pretty bad."

Fat drops of blood have painted the sink.

"You're bleeding."

"No shit."

I yank a few paper towels from the dispenser and hold them out. "Here. Let me help you."

"I don't need help," she says through her teeth, but her face is pale and scrunched up with pain.

I pull the paper towels back, unsure of myself. Should I believe her and leave? Let her deal with this herself? I can't do that.

"We should see how bad it is. What if you need stitches?"

Sucking air through her teeth, she finally loosens her grip, revealing sodden gauze. I guess Gabe tried to staunch the blood. It's not working, though. Bright red blood wells to the surface of a cut that looks about an inch and a half long. It's impossible to tell how deep, but it's bleeding a lot more than a simple paper cut.

I give her the paper towels. "Put pressure on it, okay?"

"Holy balls, it hurts!" she finally manages. Her eyes meet mine in the mirror. "God, I can't believe how stupid I am."

"Hey," I say, smiling slightly, "at least you didn't smash a bunch of carts into a car today."

She laughs once, but there's no humor in it.

"I think you might need stitches," I say as a rivulet of blood escapes from her grip and winds around to her wrist.

"It'll be fine."

"It doesn't look fine."

"I just need to tape it up or something." She winces.

"I'll get the first-aid kit." It's in the Break Room, behind a cabinet door with a huge red cross on it. I grab it, glad nobody's there to ask me what it's for. I have a feeling Sammi wouldn't appreciate me spreading the news about her injury. The only people sounds I hear are coming from the Count Out room. The deep rumble is probably Mr. Solomon, but I'm not sticking around to find out. I hurry back to the bathroom with my tackle box of medical supplies.

"Tape!" I announce, as I push the door open. "All kinds of good stuff in here."

"Thanks," Sammi says without looking at me.

I open the box and sort through all the likely

compartments until I find some packets of gauze, some tape, and some butterfly bandages. I've seen them used before on flatter areas, like my brother's forehead, but maybe they'll work.

It takes a little creativity, but eventually Sammi and I have her thumb pretty well bandaged. I still think she needs stitches, but she's adamant about not mentioning this to Kris, which we'd have to do if she went to the ER. Unfortunately, to get enough gauze and tape on to stop it from oozing, her thumb is kind of buried in a miniature cast.

"You all right like that?" I ask.

She wiggles her thumb. It only moves from the base. "Guess I have to be."

"You should tell Gabe you're okay," I say. "He looked pretty worried."

She looks down. "Yeah, maybe."

I squint at her. "What happened?"

"I told you. Box cutter."

"No, with Gabe. He seemed really upset."

"Whatever. He shouldn't have—" She clamps her lips shut and looks away from me. "He'll get over it."

I busy myself with cleaning up the scraps left from all the first-aid stuff. "You'll probably have a scar," I say instead of anything I want to say.

Our eyes meet again for a moment, and I could swear she looks relieved. "I hope it's a good one." She laughs. "I'll definitely need a better story to go with it than being clumsy with a box cutter. Something kick-ass, like a shark bite."

"You know what they say. Chicks dig scars."

Sammi looks at me in the mirror again and smirks. "Sometimes you're kind of funny."

I have no clue how to take that.

A woman comes into the bathroom with a plastic GoodFoods bag in one hand. She doesn't acknowledge us as she walks past the sinks and disappears into a stall.

I finish cleaning up the debris and try to neaten up the supplies before I close the first-aid kit. Sammi uses her unbandaged hand to splash a little water on her face and rake her bangs back into some kind of order.

From inside the stall where the customer went, we hear the sound of the plastic bag rustling. Emergency tampon run, I think. Then, I hear the distinct sound of a hard plastic container being popped open. There is nothing quite like the sound a deli container makes. I'd know it blindfolded after working in this place.

A few seconds later, there's the squeak and *poof!* of a

person opening a bag of chips. I turn to look at the stall now. What is going on in there?

I have my answer when I hear the first crunch.

Someone is eating in the bathroom. In a stall. Is she sitting on the toilet?

I look back at the mirror, meeting Sammi's eyes. She presses her lips into a tight line and gives me a look that says she's going to die of pent-up laughter. I'm not ready to laugh, exactly. I think I've been struck dumb.

*Oh my God!* Sammi mouths.

*Should we go?* I mouth back.

*Hell no!* She shakes her head. *I have to see this weirdo.*

And frankly, I kind of do, too. I mean, I'm all for politeness and letting people go about their business, but this is too weird for words.

It takes a few minutes, during which we can hardly stand to make eye contact for fear of bursting into laughter, but soon enough we hear the woman packing up the deli box and rolling the bag of chips. After that, a new sound, the metallic crack of a bottled drink cap. Then, the toilet flushes and the woman comes out.

She's older, in her forties maybe. She's wearing heels, dress pants, and a shiny blouse of some kind, and her hair looks glossy and smooth like a shampoo commercial. Not exactly what I would picture for someone who eats a meal in a public bathroom stall.

I watch as she walks to the sink area and washes her hands, then takes a moment to fix her already-perfect hair. Her eyes find mine in the mirror a few times, but I get the impression she's pretending we're not here. Sammi, on the other hand, seems to be doing her best to make sure Toilet Eater is completely aware of us.

When she finishes primping, she opens the plastic bag and pulls out the deli container I heard. It's from the prepared-foods section, a seven-layer fiesta dip thing. Basically, four kinds of fat in multicolored layers with tomatoes, green onions, and olives on top. Half of it is gone. She pitches the uneaten portion into the garbage, along with the remains of a bag of tortilla chips. Next out of the bag is a small, flat bottle of peppermint schnapps. It's also partially gone.

She looks at us in the mirror one more time. "Don't judge me. I'm having dinner with my in-laws," she says, like that explains everything. Then she unscrews the cap, takes a healthy swig, and grimaces in the mirror while she swallows.

I don't respond, but Sammi speaks up. "I sliced my thumb with a box cutter," she says. "It's just that kind of day."

"How old are you?" the woman asks.

"Nineteen," Sammi says. For a second, I wonder if that's true, but then I realize she's lying. I'm such an idiot sometimes.

Toiler Eater shrugs. "Close enough." She holds out her bottle of schnapps to Sammi. "Merry Christmas."

Then she leaves the bathroom, the plastic bag dangling from one finger. It's nearly empty now, except for the distinctive outline of a wine bottle.

I look at the bottle of schnapps.

I look at Sammi.

"On the one hand, I am holding free booze," she says. "On the other hand, it has been given to me by a person who eats dip in a public bathroom."

"Seems kind of gross to me," I say.

Sammi doesn't respond, but she slides the bottle into her apron pocket along with her bandaged thumb. We walk out of the bathroom together and head for the Break Room to put the first-aid kit away. Inside we find a few people on lunch break, Micah among them. He's the only Youngling I haven't seen since the store opened.

Sammi slides into a chair next to him. He looks distinctly nervous. I can't blame him.

"Micah, alcohol is a disinfectant, right?" she asks.

Micah is our resident genius.

"Yes," he says.

"So, there wouldn't be any germs in a bottle of alcohol?"

"Do you mean rubbing alcohol?"

"No, like the kind you drink."

"Well, that depends . . ."

She holds up a hand. "Never mind. The first answer was good enough."

"Why do you want to know?"

"No reason. Carry on." She gets up and goes to her locker, careful to keep her back to the rest of the people in the room.

I glance at the Count Out room. "Are they still in there?"

"Who? Mr. Solomon?" Micah asks. I nod. "No, they came out a few minutes ago."

"What'd they say?"

"Nothing to me. But they had the big check." He looks reflective for a moment. "It was really big."

"Hmm." I'm more curious about how much the check was for than how big it was. More than that, I can't help wondering how much it would have been for if there weren't money missing. "Did they say how much money was in the box?"

"Sixty-seven dollars."

"Hmm," I say again. "Zaina said she put in twenty dollars every time she worked. There should have been more than that. A couple hundred at least, right?"

"How many times has she worked?" Micah asks.

"I'm not sure. Maybe three times a week? That's what I work."

"Sixty dollars a week times, we'll say, seven weeks, is four hundred and twenty dollars." Micah speaks in a flat tone I've never heard him use before, his eyes rolled up toward the ceiling and his fingertips tapping out unseen code on the table. "There were sixty-seven dollars in the box this morning. Since we know Zaina put in her money this morning, and there were no other twenties in the box, let's assume the money was taken just prior to this morning. If we take Zaina's twenty away, that's an average of forty-seven dollars over a three-hour period, give or take. The store is open for an average of twelve hours a day. . . ."

I find myself leaning back, a little startled by his human-calculator routine.

And he's still talking. ". . . that's approximately one hundred eighty-eight dollars a day. Today is the twenty-fourth of December, plus how many days in November . . . ?" He seems to be asking himself, but after a long pause he looks down from the ceiling and looks at me expectantly. "How many days in November was the box up?"

"Uh . . . ," I stammer. "Didn't it go up right after Halloween?"

Micah's eyes go back to the ceiling. "So, twenty-four plus thirty is fifty-four, times a hundred and eighty-eight is—" His fingers still on the table, his open mouth soundless.

"What?" I ask.

"There could have been over ten thousand dollars in there."

MEMO–MEMO–MEMO–MEMO–MEMO–MEMO–MEMO

TO: ALL EMPLOYEES

THEFT AFFECTS ALL OF US!
What should you do if you witness
  a customer or fellow employee
  stealing?
DO:
• Report it immediately to your shift
  or store manager!
• Call the police if the thief is
  attempting to flee!
• Cooperate with an armed robber! We
  don't want our employees and valued

customers getting hurt!
- Complete an INCIDENT REPORT (obtained from your shift manager)!
- Keep your personal belongings locked in your assigned locker at all times!

DON'T:
- Attempt to apprehend the thief yourself!
- Put off reporting the incident!
- Falsely accuse your fellow employees! Theft is a serious crime, and we take all reports seriously.
- Share your locker code or cashier ID number with anyone!
- Bring large amounts of cash or valuables to work!

Ten thousand dollars? I would have expected a thousand. Maybe two thousand if people were really generous. But ten thousand? I wonder if anyone else realizes how much money is possibly missing.

Should I tell someone? I wonder. Then again, what

would I tell them? That a girl who doesn't talk much and the weird homeschooled kid who's good at math think there could be ten thousand dollars missing? Yeah. Sounds like a good way to get myself labeled a conspiracy nut.

Maybe if I had some proof . . . but what? And when did I turn into Nancy Drew, for God's sake? I think I took my distraction technique at the register a little too far. Too much time to think and too many borrowed mystery novels: that's what my problem is.

And yet, I find myself staring at the door to the Count Out Room. Could there be some kind of proof on the box itself?

I can't believe I'm even thinking about this. Besides, the room is sure to be locked.

I need an excuse for someone to let me in.

*What?* my brain demands as clearly as if someone had spoken aloud. *You are not a detective. Stop thinking crazy thoughts.*

Kris is the obvious choice.

*Correction: going back to work is the obvious choice.* So I head to the main store. But then I start scanning the registers and Customer Service for signs of Kris. My eyes find Gabe still running my register, which surprises me for a second before I remember him taking over when I followed Sammi into the bathroom. Amazing how ten thousand dollars can drive other thoughts from your mind.

Kris is doing an override at lane ten, so I slink past my own register, hoping Gabe won't notice me leaving him in the lurch. He doesn't, and neither does Tyson.

For once, I'm glad Tyson doesn't have the kind of radar for me that I do for him.

When Kris is done, I flag him down.

"What's up, Red?"

"I need quarters." It's not a bad excuse once I hear myself say it.

"Why didn't you put your light on?" He squints down the row to my register.

"I, uh, had to go to the bathroom. Gabe took over for me for a second. I figured I could just bring the roll of quarters back with me. Save some time."

"All right, come on." Kris takes off at a near-run toward the Break Room. I have to jog to keep up with him. The coded door is nearly shut behind him by the time I catch it with my fingertips. He's already at the Count Out Room door, working a key on a sizable ring into the lock.

As I wait behind him, my pulse picks up again. I have to get a look at the box quickly and without him noticing. It'll only take a few seconds for him to get me a roll of quarters.

I just hope the box is in there. With my hands stuffed in my apron pockets, I feel less childish crossing all my fingers.

Kris gets the door open. Instead of standing in the door with it propped against my foot, like I usually do, I step all the way into the room and let the door close behind me.

The big, wrapped box is there. Sitting on the desk in one corner of the small room. Kris is working on the safe, so I go straight to the desk and lean down to inspect the box's padlock, which is still in place. I lift it up to check the keyhole. There are a few faint scratches around it, but nothing that makes me think it's been jimmied with crude tools. That doesn't exclude picking, though. The whole point of picking is to make it impossible to tell a lock has been opened, isn't it? Not that I'm an expert on lock picking. Still, I'd think a screwdriver or whatever would have left at least some sign.

Then again, I'm basing all of this on the movies.

Scanning the rest of the box quickly, I don't notice any imperfections in the wrapping paper. Even after being handled today, it's still perfectly creased and taped. So either it was rewrapped after the money was stolen, or it was never damaged.

The heavy sound of the safe door shutting makes me turn my attention back to Kris.

He holds out a roll of quarters to me. "There you go, Red."

"Thanks." I slip the heavy cylinder into my apron pocket beside my notebook. "So, what was the grand total for Full Hearts Full Plates?" I ask. "I missed the big-check part."

"Oh, I don't know." He shrugs. "I've been running around so much, I barely noticed it was happening."

I can believe that. He's sweating. In December.

I offer him a smile. "Sorry they're working you so hard today."

"Hey, it's Christmas Eve. I knew what I was in for. This ain't my first rodeo."

I smile a little bigger at the dorky expression. "Anything I can do to help?"

"Get Gabe off your register before he screws up the totals and keeps me here late." He grins.

I'm about to do just that, but then the Big Mouth center in my brain takes over. "Why did you let him be a cashier anyway?"

Kris shrugs again. "Sometimes the Powers That Be make mysterious decisions."

"I take it you didn't have any say in that decision?"

He leans in like we're sharing a secret. "I don't have a say in much around here."

"Really?"

"I know, right?" He laughs. "Am I crushing your dreams of rising to the level of middle management at a regional chain of grocery stores?"

Now I'm the one laughing. "Yeah. How dare you!"

His laugh fades and he looks at me sadly. "Promise me you've got bigger aspirations than this place, Red."

I nod, even though I'm not really sure what my aspirations are. So far the only things in life that get me jazzed are good books, making lists, and Tyson's smile. Not much to build a career on.

"Good," Kris says, having no clue that my head is full of doubt. "Now get at it." He nods toward the door.

I open my mouth to tell him about Micah's math tricks and how much money I think is missing, but suddenly it seems even stupider than before. So I just smile a little and head back for the floor with my fist in my apron clutching my roll of quarters.

# MY TOP FIVE WEIRDEST THINGS TO EVER HAPPEN IN GOODFOODS MARKET*

*A Work in Progress

5. The woman who put her dog in a dress and drove her around the store sitting in the child seat. When Kris tried to enforce the "No Dogs" policy, the woman claimed the dog was a service dog that helped with her depression.
4. The man who came in dressed in a silver suit, said he was from the future, and demanded to know where we kept the nutrition tablets.
3. The man who paid his entire grocery bill—$215.56—in coins.
2. The stocker who quit in the middle of his shift after setting off a cherry bomb in a gallon of milk.

And the latest addition: 1. The woman who ate chips and dip in the bathroom stall, then gave half a bottle of peppermint schnapps to Sammi.

Before I get to Gabe, he's already talking. "Jesus, that took long enough! Is Sammi okay?"

I've never seen him look so serious.

It takes me a second to clear my head of my conversations with Micah and Kris. "She'll be all right. I think she should have had stitches, but she doesn't want to go to the hospital."

Gabe reads the total on his screen to the customer, then turns back to me as the woman goes through the card-swipe/PIN-code thing. "Did she seem . . . mad?"

"She was pretty mad about cutting herself."

"But nothing else?"

"I don't think so." I'm not getting involved in whatever went down back there, no matter how curious I am. Sammi may have thawed toward me a bit today, but I'm still pretty sure she would eagerly beat me senseless if I interfered in her personal life.

Gabe huffs out a sigh and stabs the credit button on the register to finish the transaction.

"We didn't really talk much," I say. I feel like I have to

justify my lack of information on Sammi's state of mind. "Besides, this weird woman came in and we sort of got distracted."

"Weird how?"

I wait until the customer at the register takes her receipt and moves down the lane. The next customer is unloading a pretty full cart so we'll have a moment to talk. Still, I don't want to anyone to overhear me gossiping about customers, so I lean closer to Gabe and speak in a low voice.

"She was eating southwestern bean dip in the bathroom stall. And drinking peppermint schnapps right out of the bottle."

Gabe's eyes light up. "That is without a doubt the best thing I've heard all day."

"Oh, come on, it's better than that. Top ten, for sure."

"All-time?" He looks impressed. Although I would be willing to bet no one else has a written list they keep on hand like I do, most people who work at GoodFoods have a mental tally of the weirdest things they've ever seen on the job.

Well, maybe not Agnes.

Gabe, who likes to make a game out of nearly everything, talks about his list a lot.

I consider his question. "Possibly."

"That's bold."

Mentally, I run over my list. It's only five items long so far, because I haven't seen enough things that I think deserve All-Time status. Between me and the other Younglings, though, there's more than enough stuff to make a fantastic Top Ten, but I don't think I've achieved List Collaboration status with anyone.

"I can take the register back," I remind Gabe.

"I know." He keeps scanning items. "They're trying to make me go to Produce, though, and I don't want to."

"Why not?"

"I hate stocking wet stuff. It's nasty."

I push my glasses up and stare at him.

He sighs. "Fine."

When he steps off the cushioned black mat, I take his place and finish the order he started. He doesn't go straight to Produce, of course, since this is Gabe Rossi we're talking about. He makes the most out of his walk the few feet down the aisle to Tyson's area, practically strolling.

"You up for a game of Guess the Groceries?" he asks.

"Am I ever?" Tyson replies.

Guess the Groceries is a game we all play, but Gabe is the only one who likes to do it for money. Basically, you look at a customer as they come in, and guess what they're going to buy based on how they're dressed and how they act. It's surprisingly easy.

Like Mrs. Hudson from earlier, in her high-end workout clothes. She's obviously going to go for the healthy foods. Kind of a no-brainer.

White mom types buy all the typical kid stuff: bananas, apples, carrots, cereal, hot dogs, and stuff like that.

Single women in business clothes buy diet soda, salad kits, wine, and frozen dinners.

Single men spend their money in the meat and liquor departments.

Stereotyping? Yeah, but it passes the time.

The challenge is finding someone who doesn't give you many clues. I'm pretty good at the game, if I do say so myself.

"That one." Gabe points to a customer rounding the frozen-food cases. I cringe at his blatant point, but the woman doesn't see him.

The unofficial rules of Guess the Groceries state that you cannot play with a customer who already has items in his/her cart, unless you can't see what's inside. The crowds today make it hard to see more than one or two people away, so it's a fair bet that neither of them can make out what she's pushing around in her cart.

I look, too, even though I'm not officially playing.

The target is a middle-aged woman. Everything about her screams "suburban mom." She probably has one of those stick-figure family decals in the back window of her minivan.

"A dollar says the only fruit she's got is bananas and apples," Gabe says. He likes to maximize each betting opportunity by making multiple wagers on one person.

"No bet," Tyson says, "but she's getting potatoes, too."

I'm pretty sure they're both wrong. This woman is like a version of my mom. She's probably been planning Christmas for weeks. It's not likely she's here for the usual stuff. I'm guessing she's forgotten a few things on an earlier trip, or she's here for something that has to be fresh, like shrimp or lobster.

"Interesting . . ." Gabe wanders casually down the row of registers until he can get a clear view of her. I know he'll get the answer, so I turn my attention back to my customer.

A few minutes later he comes back, and declares, "Sweet potatoes. Close, but no cigar!"

"You were wrong, too," I remind him.

"True. All right, who's next?"

I can't help it; I look for another target. A young blond woman rounds the corner into my field of vision. Her hair is full and smooth, her makeup just right. She has tall boots over her jeans and she's talking on her phone.

"Her," I say.

Gabe looks around me to the target. "Ooh, very nice. I'd buy her groceries." He grins.

I make a face at him, and Tyson punches him in the arm. "You say that about every woman under thirty who comes into this place."

"That is not true," he protests. "I don't like the crusty vegans with dreads."

Tyson shakes his head. "Gotta have standards, right?"

"Exactly."

"All right, what's she buying?" Tyson asks.

"That is a wine buyer, for sure. No food need apply."

"That was a gimme," Tyson says.

"Fine. Don't let Chloe pick anymore."

"I'm not even playing!" I protest, startling my customer, who didn't realize I was listening to the conversation at the end of the lane. "Sorry."

She goes back to her smartphone without comment.

"Who's next?" Gabe rubs his hands together like a happy villain.

Tyson shrugs. "Don't care. You pick."

"You're not making this very fun for me," Gabe says.

"We're supposed to be working."

"Exactly my point."

"You guys, how much room do you think ten thousand dollars in cash would take up?" I ask, drawing blank looks from both of them.

"What?" Gabe says.

"Like, how big do you think it would be?" I pantomime a largish cube shape in the air.

"Depends on what kind of bills you're talking about," Tyson says. "It would only be ten thousand-dollar bills." He pinches an invisible stack of bills, his fingers less than a centimeter apart.

"Mixed, I guess." I consider that. "Mostly small bills."

"Chloe," Gabe says in a fake serious voice, "are you secretly a drug dealer?"

I frown at him. "I was just thinking about the missing money."

Gabe blinks at me. "Why? Who cares?"

"Chloe likes mysteries. She's always reading them at lunch," Tyson says, and I get the warm fuzzies all over. He remembers something about me! I have to look away and scan groceries for a moment to prevent myself from blushing all over.

Just then Gabe's walkie-talkie crackles and we all hear

his name. He scoops it off his belt and keys the mic. "This is Gabe."

Kris's voice sounds strange and muffled through the walkie-talkie. "Give Chloe her lunch break. You can take yours when she's back."

"Ten-four, good buddy," Gabe says with a country twang. Then he grins at me. "So much for Produce!"

"Procrastination wins again," Tyson jokes.

"You know it." Gabe is already moving up the lane to take his position.

"But I just got back," I say.

"And?" Gabe says.

"I feel like all I've done today is hand over my register to you," I say.

"It's not my fault you have such a lousy work ethic."

I roll my eyes at him. "Don't screw up my totals."

"I'll try."

## THE FIVE PEOPLE YOU MEET IN THE BREAK ROOM DURING LUNCH

1. The Phone-Obsessed. Can be observed standing in the corner, talking loudly on phone, seemingly oblivious to the fact that the rest of us can hear everything they're saying about their sister's "worthless, broke-ass husband."

2. The Oversharer. Similar to the Phone-Obsessed, this luncher will take any opportunity to share every detail of their personal lives with anyone who will listen, often sharing things that everyone in the room wishes they could bleach out of their brains.

3. The Big Eater. There is no time for talking as far as this luncher is concerned. He packs his lunch in a full-size grocery bag or small cooler and puts down more food than most people eat in a week, all within fifteen minutes.

4. The Dieter. Always picking at a large salad or heating up a Lean Cuisine in the microwave with a dejected expression. Often goes in search of something more filling and satisfying after the pitiful lunch she packed for herself. (See also: the Afternoon Candy Breaker.)
5. The Reader. Never seen without a book or magazine, the Reader gives off a strong don't-talk-to-me vibe that only The Oversharer is ignorant to.

There aren't many people left in the Break Room when I go in for my lunch, so I haul everything out of my locker to find the paperback book I left here for company. When I first started, I pictured myself having relaxing lunches with my coworkers. We'd laugh; we'd trade stories; we'd be friends. But it turns out everyone eats on a staggered schedule so the store can still run efficiently, and most of the time the people I do eat with are not exactly friend material. So, I started bringing a book to leave at work. At least there's always something to read.

I'm really working my way through my mom's paper-back mystery collection, so I guess that's something. Something antisocial and vaguely depressing, maybe, but it's something.

Don't get me wrong: I love reading. I always have. A

good number of my lists are devoted to my favorite books, characters, and authors. But when reading yet another Sherlock Holmes mystery is all you have to look forward to at lunch, it's time to reevaluate your social life.

Nevertheless, Sherlock does his usual work of sucking me in, so I'm totally absorbed in my reading, and I don't realize at first that I can hear someone talking on the phone in the Manager's Office. I'm not even that close to the door, but whoever is talking is agitated. My ears perk up instinctively. Usually, this kind of eavesdropping would be duller than multiplication tables, but with the missing money on my mind I can't help tilting my head for a better listen.

I realize I might be able to hear even more if I were closer to the door. I bookmark my page and abandon the ubiquitous turkey sandwich my mom made me to slink closer and do some careful listening. There are a couple other people in the room, though, so I have to be casual. First step, find a plausible cover, which I do in the form of the large bulletin board mounted next to the office door. It's got all manner of boring crap posted, but the important thing is that there are enough pieces of paper up there to give me legitimate browsing time.

I can't get every word without pressing my ear to the

door, but I can at least tell that I'm listening to one side of a phone call. I squeeze my eyes shut, concentrating. ". . . security tapes show . . . certain as I can . . . sure the police . . . another employee suggested . . . yes, six of them . . . minors . . . might be working together . . ."

My heart thumps against my chest. *Minors?* Does he think we had something to do with the money?

The voice behind the door rises to a higher pitch as he ends his call, and suddenly the office door opens. I jump back, letting out a little involuntary shriek.

"Oh, I'm sorry, young lady!" It's Mr. Solomon, the district manager. He looks at me with renewed interest. "It's Chloe, right?"

"Yes." My voice fails, so I clear my throat and try again. "Yes."

"You know, it's a funny thing. I need to speak with you, and here you are!" He seems pleased with this happy coincidence.

I am not.

"I'm on my lunch break," I manage to say, one hand wavering vaguely toward the table where I left my food.

He smiles. "Perfect timing, then."

No. No, Solomon, this is not perfect timing. "Okay," I croak, and follow him into the Manager's Office.

I haven't been in here since the end of my orientation. It's a small, windowless room with a big metal desk and half a dozen corkboards on the walls. There are various binders lined up on a low bookshelf. I remember having to find some of those binders during my orientation scavenger hunt: the Emergency Preparedness Binder, the Hazmat Binder, and the Vacation Request Binder.

Solomon sits in the rolling chair behind the desk. It squeaks beneath him, sounding alarmingly like a guinea pig, and I can't help picturing a little furry creature trapped inside the cushion. He gestures for me to take the blue plastic chair at the desk's side. I do, and find myself looking at a series of posters about hand washing, ergonomics, and preventing back injuries. They all feature a little black figure like the one on a men's-room door.

That guy gets around. And he doesn't know much about safety.

Solomon folds his hands on the desk and leans toward me slightly. I fight the instinct to pull back. "Chloe, thank you for coming in," he says.

"You're welcome." Like I had a choice in the matter.

"I want to start by thanking you in advance for your cooperation. Mr. Lincoln tells me you're a model employee."

It takes me a minute to realize he means Kris. I'm also

thrown by the conversational way Solomon is talking to me, considering he most likely suspects me of stealing.

"Do you like working here?" he asks.

"Yes. Very much," I whisper. Okay, that last part might be a bit of an exaggeration, but I don't think he's looking for honesty on the subject. Who really likes their job that much?

Maybe Agnes.

"You know how we value our customers here, don't you, Chloe?" he asks.

I wish he would stop saying my name so much. "Yes," I agree.

"And you know they put their trust in us as an organization. People have a lot of choices when it comes to food shopping. They come to GoodFoods Market because they like what we have to offer. Isn't that right?"

"And the deli is awesome," I blurt out. *What?* I want to cover my hot face with my hands. What is wrong with me?

Solomon just smiles and leans even closer, like we're sharing a secret. "It is good, isn't it?"

I nod, but only a little.

Solomon continues, "Our customers put their trust in us. They trust us to maintain standards of cleanliness in our food-prep areas. They trust us to keep the floors free from spills, and parking lots free of ice that could put them in danger. They trust us to give them the best possible prices—"

My mom would definitely have something to say about that. She thinks this place is overpriced.

Solomon is still talking. "And they trust the company. They trust in our mission."

"Okay," I say.

"As I'm sure you know, that trust has been violated. In a terrible, saddening way."

I hate the way he's drawing this out. He's making me feel nervous even though I know exactly what he's getting at. My palms are starting to sweat, and I rub them on my thighs.

"Do you know what I'm talking about?" he asks.

I do. But I can't help thinking of the cart incident, and a little bit of guilt comes back to nip at me. *Focus, Chloe.* Great, now he's got me overusing my own name. I sit up as best I can. "I—I—" I stammer.

"Chloe, is there something you'd like to tell me?" he says in a hard tone.

"No."

Which goes over about as well as a chocolate-broccoli pie.

"No?" His tone of voice says it all. He thinks I'm guilty. And I am, but not of what he thinks I am.

"You're sure there's nothing you want to tell me?" he asks.

"I'm sure."

Solomon sighs. "Chloe, I have to say I'm a little disappointed. I was expecting honesty from you."

I look at my feet, noticing the water stain on my shoes from stepping in one of the slush puddles earlier. "I am being honest."

"Okay, then. I'll just ask you a couple more questions and we'll be through here. Did you observe anything unusual today?"

I blink at him. "It's Christmas Eve, Mr. Solomon. There's been some weird stuff happening."

"Such as?"

"Well, at least three different Santas came in for lunch, and we sold out of anchovies, which is weird because I never even knew we sold anchovies, and it's not like that's one of those foods you really think of when you think of Christmas, but all of a sudden everyone was buying them today and we ran out. That's pretty weird, don't you think? Is that what you're asking for?" I could go on. It's been a weird day, even by GoodFoods standards.

He shakes his head. "No. Did you see anyone near the donation box?"

"I honestly wasn't paying attention to it before you came in. But I've seen people put money in if that's what you mean."

"Any employees?" he asks.

"Zaina puts some in every time she works."

Solomon's face brightens. "Zaina Malak?"

Nodding, I wonder how many Zainas he thinks work at the store.

"Is there anything else you'd like to tell me?"

This wouldn't be a bad time to tell him that Micah estimated how much money is missing. But I just shake my head.

"Thank you, Chloe."

I leave the room slowly. The door isn't quite shut behind me when I hear Solomon click on his walkie-talkie. "Kris, would you send Zaina Malak in here?" he says.

I have to tell the others what I heard.

FIVE THINGS THAT MIGHT DESCRIBE YOU IF YOU START
CREEPING AROUND LISTENING TO OTHER PEOPLE'S PHONE
CALLS AT WORK
1. Bored
2. Nosy
3. Anxious
4. Paranoid
5. Actually being accused of a crime you didn't commit

Tyson and Gabe are right where I left them, and Zaina is
still at her register, too.

"I have to tell you guys something!"

"What's up?" Tyson asks.

"I was just in the Break Room and I overheard Mr. Solomon on the phone. He thinks one of us stole the money."

"What?" Gabe asks.

I know I shouldn't be talking about this where customers can hear, but Solomon has Kris coming for Zaina now. I don't have much choice.

"Why would he think that?" she asks. "I'm the one who gave money."

"I don't know. I just know what I heard, and when he found me outside the office he took me inside to ask me a bunch of questions."

"Did he actually accuse you of taking it?" Tyson asks.

"No. But I know he thinks we did it!"

"Who, exactly?" Gabe wants to know.

"I heard something about six minors. I think he means the Younglings."

"I'm not a minor," Gabe says. He never misses an opportunity to remind us that he's already eighteen.

"Does Solomon know that?"

He looks at me like I'm crazy. "How should I know?"

Kris's voice interrupts us. "What is going on over here?" he demands. "Gabe, there is a customer right in front of you! Tyson, bag. Chloe, what are you supposed to be doing?"

"I just got off my lunch break."

He points to where Gabe is standing. "Then get back

to work. Come on, you guys. I hate it when you make me be a hard-ass."

"Kris, Mr. Solomon just pulled me into his office to ask me about the missing money."

He shrugs. "He's talking to everybody."

"I think he thinks one of us did it." I gesture to include the others. "Sammi and Micah, too."

Kris cocks his head. "Well, did you?"

"No!"

"Then you don't have anything to worry about. Get. To. Work."

It's the harshest he's ever spoken to me, and reactionary tears prickle the back of my eyes. Shoot. I blink rapidly and squeeze past a cart to take my place back at the register.

Kris sighs and adds, "Please," before he heads off to his next task.

Amazing how one little word can change everything.

"You can go now," I say softly to Gabe.

He steps out of my way, but pauses just off the black mat beneath my feet. "I'm sure Kris is right. Solomon's probably talking to everyone."

I shake my head. "I'm serious, Gabe. He thinks one of us did it."

Gabe's walkie-talkie squawks, then Kris's voice is a

doubled blur as he talks through the speaker from the end of the lane. "Gabe. Go help the stockers in Frozen Foods. Now."

Gabe makes a face. "Well, I'm definitely being punished."

Then Kris calls up to Zaina. "Turn off your light, and total out, Z. You need to go see Mr. Solomon in the office."

Zaina doesn't respond, or even turn to look at him, but her hand goes up to flip the switch on her lighted lane number.

I look desperately at Tyson. I need one of them to believe me. He's watching Zaina, though, and doesn't meet my eyes for a second. When he does, all I get is a little half smile.

"You'll be fine," he says. "We're almost done for the day."

There is something going down here; I'm sure of it. How can I have so many bits of information and still be so clueless?

GREAT MOMENTS OF CLUELESSNESS IN HISTORY

1. On July 4, 1776, King George VI of England writes in his diary, *Nothing important happened today.*

2. The string quartet continues playing while the *Titanic* sinks.

3. In 1963, President John F. Kennedy declares, "Ich bin ein Berliner" to a roaring crowd in Berlin, Germany. Translation: "I am a jelly donut."

4. During a visit to a school, Vice President Dan Quayle corrects a student's spelling of potato as P-O-T-A-T-O-E.

5. When Pepsi expands to the Chinese market, their slogan "Pepsi brings you back to life" translates to "Pepsi brings your ancestors back from the grave."

6. Chloe Novak tries to convince her coworkers they are being accused of a crime, but no one believes her, erasing all her (possible) progress toward making actual friends at work.

Zaina doesn't come back. I don't worry about it at first, but the longer she's gone it's kind of hard not to. What could be the holdup?

"Where is she?" I ask Tyson when he comes back from cart duty yet again.

"Who?" He uses the back of his arm to blot water from his hairline.

"Zaina. She still hasn't come back."

He shrugs. "Maybe they had her do some special job." Occasionally, we get assigned to strange one-time duties, like unfolding crepe-paper turkeys for holiday displays, or taping up giant paper sneakers for some local charity fund drive.

I bite my lip. It's hard to imagine she's been asked to do something special when we know for a fact that Solomon wanted to talk to her in his office. "Do you really think so?"

"I don't know what to think." He licks one fingertip and uses it to get a stubborn plastic bag to open. "I've been too busy to worry about it."

Blood warms my cheeks. "Right. Sorry."

He sighs. "Sorry, that came out wrong."

"No, you're right. I'm obsessing." I try on a smile.

He returns one that puts mine to shame. A brilliant display of perfect white teeth, accented perfectly by his warm brown skin. My heart flutters.

I decide to go for a change of subject. "So . . . you getting anything good for Christmas?" I ask.

"Same thing I always get," he says. "College money."

"That's it?" I ask.

He nods. "Pretty much. It's all I ask for. My granny will give me something, I guess. She thinks she can knit."

"Thinks?" I echo.

"She's not real good." He grins. "I got a hat last year about this big." He hovers his hands about two inches from each side of his head.

"It's the thought that counts?" I suggest, laughing.

"She told me it's ''Cause your brains are so big.'" His slight accent gets thicker when he imitates her, and my insides melt.

"Aww. At least she appreciates that you're smart, right?"

He laughs. "That's one way to look at it."

"What'd you do with the hat?"

"My sister's dog tore it up." He shakes his head.

Kris returns before I can get any further into this story.

"Chloe. Light off and total up when you finish your customers."

I look at the long lines at every register. "Really? I'm scheduled until close."

"We're taking you off the floor. You too, Tyson."

"Why?" he asks.

"Just reshuffling things a bit," he says. "Head to the Break Room when you're done here." He moves on.

I look at Tyson.

"This is . . . different," he says.

"See? They think we did it," I say.

"Maybe. Maybe it's about something totally different."

"What else could it be?"

He drums his fingers on the end of the conveyor belt. "Um . . ."

"Exactly." I flick my light off and start moving groceries at breakneck speed. It's not like I'm in a rush to be accused of theft, but when I get nervous, I tend to do everything faster.

Overhead, the PA loops back around to "Feliz Navidad." Sure. Why not? Can't hear this song too many times.

There were three customers in my line when I turned off my light, and it doesn't take long to get through them.

With nothing left to bag, Tyson moves up the empty aisle between Zaina's and my closed registers. He grips the edges of my little enclosure and lets himself tip backward until his hands break the fall. Over and over he tugs himself back upright and then drifts into a controlled drop. I hit the keys to total up my register and wait with my fingers poised over the printer for the tape to finish spilling, trying not to watch the muscles in his forearms tense and loosen just a few inches to my right.

"So, you really think we're in trouble over this?" he asks.

"I don't know how we could be in trouble if we didn't do it, but . . . yeah, I think we're very possibly in trouble."

He licks his lips a couple times. "Did you? Take it, I mean?"

I whip my head to look at him. "No!"

"I'm just asking." He's in the pulling-up part of his cycle and he ends up looking down at me from his full height. "You can tell me."

"I didn't do it." I raise my eyes to look at him and have to push my glasses up to see. "Did you?"

"Nope. I need this job. Why would I risk it?"

"I guess you wouldn't need it as much if you stole ten thousand dollars."

He falters and has to scramble to grab the edges again. "Ten thousand?"

"Maybe."

"Is that why you were asking how big that would be before?"

"Yeah. Why did you think I was asking?"

"I don't know. I guess I thought it might have been about something in one of your books."

I tell him quickly about Micah's math gymnastics.

"But that could be too high, right?"

"Could be. It's still probably a lot more than we were thinking."

"Damn," he says softly.

The register releases my cash drawer and I lift out the till. "All right. I guess this is it."

Tyson grins. "Dead men walking?"

"I hope not."

We fall in step as soon as we're clear of the checkout lane, and we're nearly touching as we approach the Break Room. I chance a look up at him as we slow before the door.

He bumps my shoulder with his. "Hey, no sweat, right? We didn't do it; we got nothing to worry about." He doesn't look like he's completely sure about that.

But I say, "Obviously," because what else can you say?

As I enter the door code, I can't resist a last-minute prayer. *Oh, please let this be about a Christmas bonus. Or at least a Christmas cookie.* I don't know which deity might be in charge of Christmas cookies, so I send my wish out into the general universe.

Inside, Zaina sits at one of the rickety round lunch tables. She has her hands neatly folded in her lap. There are two other people in the room: Micah, who is reading a book, and Gabe, who is talking quietly on his phone in the far corner of the room.

"What's going on?" I whisper.

"Kris took my till." Zaina inclines her head toward the Count Out Room. It's completely outside of normal procedures for someone else to count your till. They made a big deal out of it during cashier training.

The little ball of dread in my stomach inflates a few sizes.

"Where's Mr. Solomon?" I ask.

"In there. With Sammi." Zaina nods at the Manager's Office with wide eyes, which is really saying something. She has huge, hazel eyes under normal circumstances.

There is a bank of counters along one wall, with a sink and the employee refrigerator. On top, I notice the black plastic trays that had been covered in Christmas cookies are all but empty. Just a few crumbs and a couple of rejected broken cookies. There's also a less-than-appealing carton of eggnog with congealed dribbles down the sides. I wonder how long it's been sitting out.

Tyson browses the trays and chooses one of the broken cookies.

Suddenly the door to the Count Out room opens and Kris appears in the gap. He sees me and laughs. "You look like someone stole your puppy."

A wheezy laugh sneaks out of me. "Sorry. I'm just nervous, I guess."

Kris lifts his hand, fingers wiggling in a "come here" gesture. "No worries. Here, I'll count your till."

I don't consider myself a complete Goody Two-shoes—take my malicious coverup of the damaged car, for example—but giving up my till makes me hesitate. A lot. Even though it's my boss telling me to do it. My fingers just don't want to ease up their grip as I extend the till toward Kris.

He looks at me, and laughs again. Not in a mean way, but I feel my cheeks get hot. "Chloe, we can let it slide this once, okay? I promise I'm a really good counter."

That makes me blush harder, and I hand it over quickly. Kris smiles at me and goes back into the room.

"Did Mr. Solomon talk to all of you?" I ask the others.

Zaina nods, and Gabe puts up one finger to indicate he's still on the phone. Micah marks his page with the jacket flap and looks up. "He thinks one of us knows something about the missing money." He sounds almost cheerful about it. Then again, Micah sounds cheerful about nearly everything.

THINGS YOU WILL LEARN ABOUT MICAH YODER WITHIN
FIVE MINUTES OF MEETING HIM

1. He is one of those people who seems to know a little bit about everything.
2. He is homeschooled.
3. He is terminally cheerful. Happier than anyone else I know. Sometimes I wonder if it's a result of #2.
4. His hair is almost as light as Sammi's but clearly natural. His eyebrows are nearly invisible, and his eyelashes are just a shade or two darker.

Gabe shoves his phone into his pocket as he approaches the table where Zaina sits. He flips one of the chairs around to straddle it and says, "So, which one of you did it?"

"None of us did it." Micah looks at all of us. "Did we?"

"I didn't," Gabe says. "Kinda wish I did, but I didn't."

"I didn't!" Micah says immediately.

"We know that." Gabe rolls his eyes. "I don't even know why he bothered putting you in here."

"I could have done it!" Micah protests. "I just didn't."

"I didn't do it," Zaina says softly.

"Neither did I," Tyson agrees.

"Me neither," I say. "So, that just leaves—"

As if on cue, the door to the Manager's Office opens and Sammi comes out, scowling.

"Sam—" Gabe starts to stand, but she ignores him and drops into the closest chair without a word. Her seat is about as far as she can get from the rest of us without leaving the room.

A moment later, Mr. Solomon emerges. "Ah. Good. You're all here." Once again he's got that conversational, "isn't this a happy coincidence" tone that doesn't fit the situation.

"Hi, Mr. Solomon," Micah says. No one else speaks.

"I'm sure you're wondering why you're here," he says after an agonizing pause.

Actually, we all know exactly why we're here. What's not clear is what he's still looking for after he talked to each of us individually.

"As you know, there's been an incident at the store. I've already spoken to each one of you about this. Unfortunately, no one has been forthcoming with the information I need to settle this matter."

Again, no one speaks. What would we even say? We've pretty much been accused of stealing and now covering it up. I've watched enough police shows to know this is the time to keep quiet.

"This is the largest GoodFoods store in the region," Mr. Solomon finally says. "The busiest. What do you think I expected to find when I opened up our donation box this morning? Why do you think *this* was the store we chose to come to last? With a *television crew*, no less?"

It's pretty obvious he's not looking for answers at this point, so we stay silent.

"Sixty-seven dollars," he continues. "We've been collecting money since November, and there are only sixty-seven dollars in this store's box."

"That's not possible," Zaina says softly.

"Precisely my point. Every other GoodFoods in this region had hundreds if not thousands of dollars in their boxes. The Fairview store alone had more than seven thousand.

"I checked the security footage. Over the last forty-eight hours, I saw dozens of customers put their hard-earned money in here. They thought they were helping out needy families at Christmastime. But a thief has violated that sacred trust. The trust our customers put in GoodFoods Market.

"I have reason to believe the culprit is among us in this room. It would be easiest for everyone if that person would step forward now."

Again, no one speaks. Solomon lets the silence stretch out, eyeballing each one of us in turn. The way he's staring makes me feel like a dog that pooped on the rug.

"I didn't want to do this. I was hoping the guilty party would realize the seriousness of their actions and come forward out of a sense of duty. If not to me, if not to the GoodFoods name, then to their coworkers."

Sammi snorts, but tries to bury it in a cough.

"Whoever did this has put all of your reputations on the line." His eyes narrow. "Unless, of course, you were working together."

Still no one speaks.

"Fine, then. If that's the way you want it. I'm going to have to contact the police." He straightens up. "You will all wait here until they arrive. We've excused you from the floor, and your work will be covered by the rest of the staff. You are not to leave this room. Do you understand? Perhaps some time to think will help you decide to give up the guilty party."

Solomon disappears into the Manager's Office, leaving us alone under the cold light of the buzzing fluorescents.

Sammi sighs. "Merry frickin' Christmas."

FIVE CRIMES I HAVE ACTUALLY COMMITTED IN MY LIFE
1. Speeding (who doesn't?)
2. Sneaking into a second movie after the one I went to let out (Eva's idea)
3. Jaywalking (again—who doesn't?)
4. Copying a friend's CD (Eva's)
5. Trespassing (in Eva's neighbor's yard to jump on their trampoline)*

   *Note: Looking back, I think Eva may have been a bad influence on me.

I don't know what the others are doing, but I'm trying to process everything that just happened. I understood the words that came out of Mr. Solomon's mouth, of course, but they didn't seem like they belonged in that particular order. Is he putting us under some kind of work arrest? Is that even possible?

The alarm on my watch sounds, but I manage to squeeze the silence button after only two chirps. It's time for another blood-sugar check, but I'm not going to interrupt everything to do it now. I feel fine.

"Well, this sucks," Sammi finally says.

"Are we, like, under house arrest or something?" Gabe wonders.

"He can't do that, can he?" Tyson looks at me, then the others. "Make us stay here, I mean?"

"He definitely can't." Sammi stands up. "And he can't do this bullshit grounding-us-at-work thing, either."

"Technically, we're still on the clock," Micah says. "So, I think he can ask us to do whatever he wants."

"This is ridiculous."

"Sammi, wait." I stand slowly. "If we just figure out who did this, we'll be out of here."

"What are you, Nancy Drew?" she says.

"It's better than sitting around waiting for the cops," I say.

"Fine." She drops into a chair. "Whoever did it just say so, okay? I don't want to be here any longer than I have to."

"Did anyone here do it?" I ask.

"How do we know you didn't do it and you're just asking the questions to mislead us?" Sammi quirks an eyebrow in challenge.

"Because I didn't do it," I answer.

"Well, neither did I," she replies.

"Me neither," Gabe says.

"It wasn't me," Zaina adds.

"I didn't take it," Tyson says.

"God as my witness, I did not take the money." Micah lays a hand on his chest.

Sammi makes a derisive sound. "Whoever did this needs to frigging confess already. I want to get out of this craphole."

"We've already established that no one here did it," Tyson reminds us.

"No, what we've established is that no one here is willing to confess," Sammi counters.

A few people groan, defeated.

"This isn't getting us anywhere," I say. "We need to figure out a way to prove we didn't do it."

"Oh, all right, you can strip-search me!" Gabe holds his arms wide.

"I'm not taking my clothes off," Micah says in all seriousness.

"Nobody's taking their clothes off!" Sammi says,

giving Gabe a stern look. I can't help but notice it's the first time she's spoken directly to him. He looks a little surprised himself, and for once, he doesn't have a snappy comeback.

"There's no way to prove we didn't do it," Zaina says. "You have to trust someone if you're going to believe them. What reason do I have to trust any of you?"

"I'll swear on a Bible," Micah says. "A stack of them!"

"No one thinks you did it, Micah." I reach out to squeeze his wrist.

"Why not? I could have."

"No, you couldn't have," Sammi says.

"Yes, I could."

"Micah, you're the kind of guy who would drive across town to give a penny back to the store if they gave you too much change," I say. He's like the Abraham Lincoln of GoodFoods.

He looks at me, confused, but I'm pretty sure it's because he can't imagine there's an alternative to that drive across town. "It would be the right thing to do."

I nod. "Exactly. There's no way you embezzled a bunch of charity money."

"I'm just saying I could have."

"No, you couldn't have," Tyson, Gabe, and Sammi say simultaneously.

Micah startles back at the loudness of their combined voices, then looks at his hands in his lap. "I did something bad once. Here at the store." He looks up without lifting his head, giving him a slightly crazed expression.

"No way." Gabe laughs.

"I did." Micah raises his head now, his face earnest.

"What?"

"I'm not sure I should say."

"Out with it." Sammi nudges his chair with her foot.

"You know how Mr. Lincoln let me try out as a cashier a couple weeks ago?" Micah is the only other person besides Mr. Solomon who calls Kris "Mr. Lincoln."

"Yeah."

"My register came out wrong."

"And?" Gabe and I exchange looks and he tilts his chair back on two legs, gripping the table for balance. Registers come out slightly off sometimes. It's not a big deal. Usually it's just a few coins.

"I must have given somebody too much change." Micah clamps his hands on his head. "It was *ten dollars* off!"

"What did Kris say?"

Micah shakes his head. "Nothing. I didn't tell him."

Gabe thunks his chair onto all four legs again. "You lied?"

I totally get his accusing tone. I can't believe it myself.

"Not exactly." Two spots of color appear on Micah's cheeks. "I put in some of my own money."

Everyone groans. "Come on, man!" Gabe protests.

"What?" Micah asks. "I didn't want to cause trouble."

"It was a mistake, wasn't it?" I clarify.

"Yes, of course."

"Then why do you think it would have been trouble?"

"It was ten dollars!" he reminds us.

"Micah, seriously," Gabe says. "It was just ten bucks."

Micah shakes his head. "It was the right thing to do."

"Yeah, there is no way you stole a bunch of charity money," Sammi says, standing up. "Micah is now the official standard of truth in this room. If you can swear on Micah's head you didn't do it, I believe you."

Taking a deep breath, she lowers her hand onto Micah's blond head, palming it like a basketball. "I solemnly swear on the head of Micah Yoder that I did not steal the charity money."

"We already established that the thief would lie," Tyson reminds her.

Growling with frustration, she shoves Micah's head as she lets go of it, then walks to the other side of the room and boosts herself onto a low counter. "We're never going to get out of here."

"Maybe we should start at the beginning." I reach into my apron to pull out my little notebook, and flip to a clean page.

"You're actually going to take notes?" Sammi says.

My cheeks burn. "I thought it would help keep it all straight."

"Oh brother."

"Go 'head, Chloe." Tyson gives Sammi a dirty look. "You were saying?"

I hesitate, but Tyson nods. "We should start at the beginning."

"In the beginning there was the Word . . . ," Gabe intones.

"A little more recent than that, dipshit," Sammi says.

"A long time ago in a galaxy far, far away?" he tries.

"How about we stick with today?" I suggest.

"Suit yourself." Gabe leans back and props his ankle on his opposite knee. "You wanna know what I had for breakfast, or should I start with when I got here?"

"How about this: Did anyone see anyone else near the money box when they arrived?" I'm asking everyone, but I focus on Zaina since she's the only one I know for sure would have gotten close to it this morning.

She shakes her head. "There was no one out there when

I put my money in the box. Then I came here to punch in."

"Anyone else?" I try the others. The only responses are negative.

"So, nobody saw anything," Gabe says in a flat voice. "Great. We've got nothing."

"We just need to think this through!" I exclaim. "We'll figure it out."

"No, we won't. Whoever did it is going to lie about it anyway. Maybe we should just let the cops come," Gabe says.

"Do you really think he's going to call the police?" Micah asks.

"Why would he lie?" Zaina asks.

"What's he going to say?" Sammi says. "'I think someone stole some money, but I don't know how much'?"

"But if he actually saw people putting money in on the security tapes . . ." Tyson taps his chin.

"The tapes only keep for forty-eight hours," she reminds him. "So, he saw a few people put money in the box. There's money in the box. Where's the crime?"

"My money is missing," Zaina reminds us. "My mother's, I mean. I put more than one twenty-dollar bill in there."

Sammi deflates. "Oh, yeah."

"It doesn't really matter if there was an actual crime. If he calls the police, they'll come," I say. "I have an aunt who calls the cops all the time. There's never been an actual crime when they got to her house."

Gabe laughs. "Seriously? Why does she call?"

"She always thinks people are trying to break into her house." I shrug. "Apparently there are a lot of unsavory characters out there interested in collectible German figurines."

"What do they do when they get there?"

"Not much. Look around for signs of a break-in. There's never been anything missing. Mostly they just tell her to call the nonemergency number unless she thinks she's in danger." I realize they're all staring at me, and my cheeks get hot again. "I guess she's kind of weird."

"I love it," Sammi says.

"So, okay, he calls the cops and they come look at the box," Gabe says. "The lock isn't broken and there's money inside. We all go home, right?"

"They could fingerprint us," I say.

"You think?" Tyson asks.

"Maybe."

"They can't do that," Sammi says. "Not if we're not under arrest."

"I think they can if we volunteer to have it done," Micah says. "I'm not up on the law."

"Fine. We get fingerprinted, and we get the hell out of here," Gabe says. "Let Solomon go ahead and call. I want to get this over with."

"No," Sammi says. "I don't want to get fingerprinted."

"Why?" Gabe says. "I don't care if they fingerprint me. I've got nothing to hide."

"Well, I care," Sammi snaps. "I don't want the Five-Oh to have my prints on file."

Gabe cocks an eyebrow. "Planning a life of crime we don't know about, Samantha?"

"Don't call me that, asshole." She flicks a paper clip at him.

"Now, now." He shakes his head sadly. "There's no need to resort to violence."

"Fine." She sticks her middle finger up at him and he grins.

"Sticks and stones may break my bones," he says in a high, squeaky voice. I'm pretty sure they're making up for whatever went down before Sammi cut herself, but it's definitely the weirdest apology I've ever seen.

Suddenly my watch starts chiming again and I slap my hand over it reflexively. Darn. I must have snoozed it before instead of shutting it off.

"What's wrong with your watch?" Micah asks.

"Nothing. It just alarms sometimes." Or, you know, every time I'm supposed to check my blood sugar.

"I can turn that off for you. I'm good with technical stuff." Micah holds his hand out to take it from me.

"It's fine." My ears are hot again, but this is the old standby heat. It'll go away if I can get them to talk about something else.

"Did anyone see anything weird today?" I ask.

Gabe barks out a humorless laugh. "You mean apart from Coupon Lady and Melon Sniffer?"

"The chick in the bathroom?" Sammi looks at me with a smirk.

"The woman with all the rice," Zaina adds.

"What woman?" Micah asks Zaina.

"Today I had a customer with twelve bags of rice and one two-liter of Dr Pepper," she says.

"Nice." Gabe's face lights up with interest. "All right, who can beat it?" He reaches in his pocket and comes out with some change. "I got . . . eighty-three cents for the weirdest purchase today." He slams his hand down on the table, making it shiver and quiver with fear. Poor table is not up to this kind of abuse. The coins stay in a small, linty pile when Gabe lifts his hand.

No one speaks up.

"Anyone? Come on. Who can beat twelve bags of rice and Dr Pepper? There's money on the line here, people!"

"All right, I got one," I say. "Diapers, a bottle of gin, cat litter, and three dozen eggs."

"Not bad, not bad . . ." Gabe nods slowly. "Who else?"

"Umm . . ." Micah opens his mouth, but then shakes his head.

"What?" Gabe asks.

"No. Never mind."

"What is it?" I ask.

"I don't know. I feel like I'm making fun of people if I play."

"You are," Sammi says, the "so what?" implied.

"But they don't know it," Gabe reasons. "Who are you hurting?"

"And we're not saying they're bad people," I say. "It's just that sometimes people buy weird combinations of things."

"I guess so."

Gabe is watching Micah. "You got something, don't you?"

"Maybe."

"Come on. Tell us," he urges.

"Are you sure?"

"Tell us," Gabe repeats in a low voice.

"I was bagging on Agnes's lane"—Micah's voice rises at the end like a question—"and there was a customer"—another questioning tone—"and he bought chicken nuggets, whipped cream, a five-pound bag of onions, and two packs of ex-lax."

"Winner!" Gabe declares, pushing the money across the table to Micah. Micah doesn't touch it, but he smiles a little.

"You guys, this isn't helping," I say. "We're supposed to be figuring out who stole the money."

"Chloe, give it a rest," Gabe says. "Nobody saw anything, and no one here is going to admit it, even if they took it. I say we wait for the cops, get fingerprinted, and get out of here."

"My fingerprints will be on the box," Zaina says. "I put money in every time I work."

"What's the deal with that anyway?" Gabe asks.

"My mother gives it to me."

"But isn't your family . . . ?" I start to ask, but immediately wish I could suck the words back in. My busted filter is at it again.

Zaina fixes her eyes on me until my cheeks are on fire. Even my ears ache from the rush of blood. I'm probably the same color as my hair at this point.

"Zaina's Muslim, Chloe." Micah gives the answer.

"That's right," Zaina confirms. "Do you suppose that makes me less charitable than you?" The calm tone and the formal speech are dead giveaways that she's angry; I'm sure of it.

"No, I . . ." I look down at my lap, wanting to die. Oh God, oh God, now everyone is going to think I'm racist. Oh God.

"She didn't mean anything by it," Tyson says.

"Didn't she?" Zaina shifts her gaze to Tyson. "Are you sure?" This might be the most I've ever heard her speak, and it is all directed at me, but not in a good way.

"I—" My voice breaks when I try to speak up. "I just meant that it's a collection for Christmas dinner. . . ."

"And?" Zaina prompts.

"Nothing. I'm sorry." My eyes sting and my nose is burning deep inside. *T minus ten seconds to tears!* my brain warns with sirens and blaring horns.

Tyson pats me on the shoulder.

"My family believes in taking care of the people of Islam *and* those of other faiths," Zaina says slowly.

"Infidels," Micah pipes up in his usual enthusiastic tone.

I gasp. I can't help it.

"Nice, Micah." Gabe groans.

"What? That's the right word."

Zaina narrows her eyes at him. "Why do you know so much about my religion?"

Micah blinks. "I know a lot about a lot of religions."

"Why?"

"I know a lot about a lot of things," he says.

Sammi bangs on the table, making Micah's eighty-three cents in prize money jump. "All right, all right. We're all so much more culturally sensitive now, blah blah blah. Can we please figure out who stole the frickin' money so I can get out of this place sometime before midnight?"

As a group, we look at the clock mounted on the wall above the printer. It reads two forty-five p.m.

"I'm supposed to go home in fifteen minutes . . . ," I say softly. My mom is going to kill me if I'm late.

"Me too," Gabe agrees.

"We all are," Sammi says.

"He's not going to keep us after the store is closed," Zaina says. "Is he?"

"No way." Sammi gets up and crosses to the Manager's

Office. She knocks on the door and doesn't wait before opening it. "Mr. Solomon, none of us did it. How long do you expect us to sit here?"

I can't see inside the office from this angle, but I can see when Sammi has to jog backward as Solomon strides out to speak to us.

"The police are on their way. I'm asking that you remain here until they arrive."

"Sir, the store is going to close in fifteen minutes," Micah says. "Are you asking us to stay after closing?"

"My mom will freak out if I'm late," I say.

"Isn't it, like, kidnapping if you keep us here against our will?" Gabe asks with an impressive look of innocence.

For the first time, Solomon looks alarmed. Not much, but I can see he hasn't thought this through. He runs his tie between two fingers and straightens the already-straight knot. "You may call your families. Tell them you've been asked to stay late. I can speak to them if you wish."

"Are you going to tell them we've been accused of stealing?" Micah asks.

"Now, now. No one's saying you did it—"

"That's exactly what you said," Sammi interrupts.

He gives her a hard look. "I'm simply asking you to stay while we wait for the police. It should be a simple

matter to eliminate your fingerprints. The more coopera-
tive you are, the faster this will go. If any of you need to use
the office phone to call home, you may do so."

As if on cue, we all pull cell phones from various pockets. Gabe and Sammi start thumb-typing, going with the
safe texting route. So much easier to get away with stuff
when you can't hear your mother's reaction. I consider it
myself, but my mom doesn't usually carry her cell around
with her. The text could sit unread for hours. She'll have
already called the police to report me missing by then.

Nope, I have to do this old-school.

I can practically hear a funeral dirge as I head to a quiet
corner to make the call.

TOP TEN WORST MOM PHRASES

10. "Young lady . . ."

9. Anything that includes your middle name

8. "I thought you were dead! Or worse!"

7. "I worry about you!"

6. "You know, when I was your age . . ."

5. "You're not going out like that, are you?"

4. "Look me in the eyes and tell me that again."

3. "If all your friends jumped off a cliff, would you?"

2. "I'm not mad. I'm just disappointed."

1. "Do what you think is right. I'm sure you'll make the right choice."

The phone call goes about as well as I expected. There's a lot of sighing and audible fretting. She's not happy. That's putting it mildly. But since it's work-related, she can't complain. Especially once I offer to put Mr. Solomon on the phone. I'm really glad she doesn't take me up on that, though. I could just picture him telling her exactly why I'm being kept late. Alleged theft would *not* sit well with the mom.

As the minute hand passes the twelve, other employees start coming in to grab their coats and punch out. It takes a while, as people finish side jobs and the last straggling customers are finally seen out of the store. Everyone stares at us.

I can't blame them. If I came into the Break Room and found six people sitting around a table at closing time, I'd wonder what was going on, too.

The first time someone asks what we're doing, Sammi answers honestly, "Waiting for the police. Apparently we're now a ring of criminal masterminds."

The asker, who is a stocker named Dave, laughs like he's not sure if she's joking.

The second time, Tyson refers them to Mr. Solomon for an explanation.

The third time, Mr. Solomon has apparently had enough, because he tells us all to go into the Manager's Office and wait for the rest of the employees to go home.

He doesn't lock us in, but it's pretty clear we're not supposed to leave. Particularly since he stations himself outside the door wishing everyone happy holidays and generally sounding like the fakest festive holiday kind of guy in three counties.

"This is such bullshit," Sammi says, sliding her back down the wall to sit between a filing cabinet and a garbage can.

"I feel like I'm in detention," Gabe says.

"More like jail," I say. "At least in detention there are enough chairs for everyone." There are only two chairs in here—the one behind the desk, which Gabe took, and the hard plastic chair. Zaina's sitting there. I've managed to hitch one hip onto the edge of a short filing cabinet. Micah and Tyson are still standing, though they've each found a spot to lean on the wall. It's crowded to the point of making me feel a little claustrophobic. My thermal shirt is way too warm with six bodies crammed into this small space.

Overhead, the PA shuts up with an abrupt click and the Christmas music is gone. I feel tension uncoil from my shoulders that I didn't even know I was holding there. Zaina and Tyson sigh with relief, too.

"About effin' time!" Sammi says in a voice loud enough

to be heard in the Break Room.

"Don't you worry that you're going to get in trouble for talking like that?" Micah asks her.

"All I said was *effing*." She looks through her bangs at him. "Don't want to offend your virgin ears and all."

"I didn't mean the swearing," Micah says.

"He means you have a bad attitude," Gabe says.

"Kiss my ass, Gabe," she says. "You don't have to, Micah."

Gabe laughs and makes a big kissy sound in the air. Micah's expression is one I would call Confused Puppy.

"Besides, someone's got to have some attitude around here. We're being held against our will in a windowless room!" she shouts, again for Solomon's benefit. "This is definitely in violation of fire codes! How are we supposed to get out of here if there's a fire?!"

No one from the outside answers.

"See?" Sammi continues. "If we don't make some noise, they'll probably leave us in here all night. We'll all suffocate and they'll find our corpses on Christmas morning. How festive!"

"Store's closed tomorrow," I remind her.

"Even better! We'll have time to start rotting. Stinking corpses on the day after Christmas!"

"All right, Sam! Jeez. Give it a fricking rest." Gabe rolls his eyes, earning a nasty look from her. "You're going to give us all hearing damage."

She opens her mouth for a retort, but I cut her off. "Zaina, did you tell Mr. Solomon how much money you put in today?"

"Of course," she says.

"And did you tell him you do it every time you work?" I'm trying to remember Micah's earlier calculations.

"I answered his questions," she nonanswers.

"Sounds kind of shady, if you ask me, Z," Sammi declares, grinning. "You sure you were putting money *in* the box?"

Zaina's head whips up, her eyes cold. "Are you accusing me of stealing?"

Sammi puts her hands up. "Relax. It was a joke."

"I don't think it's very funny."

"Oh, for God's sake."

"Why are you picking on her?" Tyson says.

"It was a *joke*." She shoves herself up from the floor and walks to the far corner of the room, which is all of three steps away. "Christ. What is the big deal?"

"You should apologize," Tyson insists.

Sammi stares at him, but Tyson meets her gaze without

hesitation. Finally, she lets out a short bark of laughter. "Oh my God, you're serious."

"Let it go, Tyce," Gabe says. "She was just joking around."

"No, no. He's right, Gabe. I mean, God forbid anyone should be offended around here, right?" Sammi clasps her hands under her chin. "Gee, Zaina, I'm awful sorry I made a joke that hurt your widdle feewings. I'm sure you've never stolen anything in your sweet, pure life!"

Zaina's jaw clenches and she looks down.

"Why do you have to be such a bitch?" Tyson says.

"Why do you have to defend her? She giving you a little action when no one's around?"

"Sammi!" Gabe says at the same time that Zaina starts to say, "You can't talk about—"

Just then the office door opens and Solomon stares at us. Everyone goes silent.

"The rest of the employees have gone home," he says. "Thank you for your cooperation."

"So we get to come out now?" Micah asks.

"Please." He gestures like he's an usher at a fancy theater.

"Finally." Sammi glares at everyone before storming past Solomon into the Break Room.

Gabe turns back to look at the rest of us, still crammed

in the office. "Z, she didn't mean anything by it."

"It's Zaina. And you shouldn't defend her all the time," Zaina says curtly before she walks out to take up a position as far from Sammi as possible.

"Sammi acts tough, but she's not actually mean." Gabe seems eager to convince at least one of us as we file out. As soon as we're clear of the door, Solomon goes inside and lets it shut behind him.

"Maybe you shouldn't talk about me when I can hear you, geniuses," Sammi says from near the bank of lockers.

"Do you ever get tired of being such a bitch all the time?" Tyson asks.

Her jaw slides to one side. "Do you ever get tired of being so fake?"

"Fake?" he repeats.

"You always act so nice. 'Thank you, ma'am,' and 'Yes, sir!' Like you're so polite and perfect. It's disgusting."

"Shut up!" The words are out of my mouth before I knew I was going to speak.

Sammi zeroes in on me. "Bite me, Red."

"Leave her alone," Tyson says.

"Oh, here we go." She rolls her eyes. "Time to be the knight in shining armor."

"Sam." Gabe speaks in a low voice.

"Stay out of it, Gabe."

"I'm just trying to be a friend."

"To who?" she demands. "To them? Or to me?"

"To all of you."

"Yeah? Well, you can leave me out of it, okay? Does that make it easier?" She slumps into a chair, face turned to avoid looking at any of us.

No one speaks. My whole body feels like it's crawling with bugs, and my stomach is churning. I hate situations like this.

I have to do something, even if it makes me look like an idiot. Anything will be better than this bath of unspent hostility.

Diving headlong into potential disaster, I ask, "How's your thumb, Sammi?"

Her eyes slide to me before her head turns. "Oh, it's fantastic. It feels so great, I'm thinking of cutting the rest of my fingers open, too."

"What happened to your thumb?" Micah asks.

"She sliced it with a box cutter," Gabe answers before she can. "Pretty bad."

"Ouch," Micah says.

"Don't talk about me behind my back." Sammi stands, glaring at Gabe.

"Actually, I'm talking about you *in front* of your back."

"Whatever." Sammi kicks her chair farther away from the table and sits mostly turned away from the rest of us. I can see the backs of all her earrings in one ear and the curve of her cheek.

"Don't be like that." Gabe taps her chair with his foot. "It's not like I told them some major secret."

"It's fine. I don't even care."

"Yeah, you sound totally over it."

She whips her head to look at him. "Why don't you just leave me alone?"

"Fine by me."

She turns away from him again, but Gabe picks up another chair and moves it around to face hers. He sits, clearing his throat and looking impassively at her.

"Do you think that's funny?" she says.

"Oh, I'm sorry, I didn't realize you were speaking to me."

"Shut up." She shifts, uncrossing her legs to give his chair a push with her foot.

He nudges his chair closer. "Excuse me, you're in my space."

"You're such an asshole," she says, but even from this oblique angle, I can see she's starting to smile.

"You're so shitty at pouting." He leans forward, elbows on knees to speak softly to her. "And it's really annoying on top of that, so could you knock it off?"

She tries to scowl at him, but fails.

I can't take my eyes off them. They're a strange pair, but Gabe actually seems to get her.

After a moment of murmured talk between them, he stands up and goes behind her chair to turn it with her still sitting in it. The rubberized feet squeal across the floor. She's trying to look pissed, but she's also trying not to laugh as he scoots her closer to the rest of us with an earsplitting *rrreeeeeeeeeee!*

"There!" he says in a cheerful, preschool-teacher voice. "Look at these nice people who are trapped in work jail with you. Don't you want to play with them?"

She twists to swat him in the stomach with the back of her hand. "God, you're such a pain in the ass."

I can't help noticing her hand as she smacks him. It's the one she cut earlier, but my awful bandage is gone. I blurt out, "Did the bandage fall off?" totally alerting them to the fact that I'm watching them like a TV show.

She shrugs, inspecting her thumb casually. "I couldn't do anything with it. Rick superglued it for me."

"What?" Tyson can't help himself; he moves toward

her for a closer look.

"Superglue?" I ask. "Is that safe?"

"Dunno, but it burns like a son of a bitch, I can tell you that," she says.

"Can I—?" Tyson holds out one hand, hesitant.

She gives him a sideways thumbs-up, revealing a row of small bandages.

"Is that okay? To use it on your skin, I mean?" I ask.

"It worked."

"Doctors in the military used superglue for lots of things during Vietnam," Micah supplies. "There's a medical grade now, but it's a slightly different chemical."

"Man, you're a nerd," Gabe says.

Micah shrugs.

"Pretty clean cut," Tyson says, inspecting her hand up close now.

"I don't fuck around." She takes her hand back and tucks it into crossed arms.

Suddenly Tyson seems to realize he's been admiring the cut of a girl he recently called a bitch. Twice. He clears his throat and steps back a few paces. "Look, Sammi, I'm—"

She shakes her head. "Just forget it."

"No, but I—"

"Seriously, forget it, okay? We're all stuck here. It's

fine." She looks at us through her bangs for a second, then down at her hands. "Sorry."

He nods. I check over my shoulder to see what Zaina's doing, but she doesn't make eye contact. She's sitting at one of the other tables, focused on a spot a few inches from her folded hands.

As much as I want to, I don't know how to break the ice with her.

"How long do you think it'll take the police to get here?" I ask, mostly for distraction.

"Somehow, this doesn't strike me as a nine-one-one occasion," Tyson says.

"I know, right?" Sammi agrees. "Quick! Come to GoodFoods, it's possible someone stole some money, but I don't know how much, or if anything was actually even stolen! Hurry!"

Gabe holds an imaginary phone up to his ear. "Uh, sir, you do realize there are consequences for making a fake call to nine-one-one?" he says in a nasally tone.

Sammi grins. "But this *is* an emergency! Send a SWAT team! There are a few twenty-dollar bills missing!" She's really hamming it up now, making Gabe laugh.

"It could be eighty, even . . . *gasp* . . . one *hundred* dollars!" he adds.

"Actually, it's probably closer to ten thousand," Micah says absently.

The room goes still. It's so quiet, I literally hear water dripping into the sink. Makes me wish I had a pin to drop.

THINGS YOU CAN DO WITH $10,000
1. Get 20,000 candy bars when they're two for a dollar.
2. Never have to beg your parents for gas money for the rest of high school.
3. Pay for half a semester at Harvard.
4. Buy a used car. (But you should definitely check if the driver's-side door opens first.)
5. Throw yourself one of those insane Sweet Sixteen parties like on TV.

Gabe is the first to recover. "What?"

"It's just an estimate, but if today's collection was any indication, it could have been that much. It was at least a few thousand."

"Are you kidding me?" Sammi half rises from her lotus

position on her chair, then sits again. "Do you know what I could do with ten thousand dollars?"

"If I had ten thousand dollars, I wouldn't be working at this place, that's for sure," Gabe says.

"Ten thousand dollars is still below the poverty line," Micah reminds him.

"Yeah, but it's a hell of a lot of pizza-and-beer money when you're living in a dorm." Gabe rubs his hands together. "Unbelievable. Well, now you know for sure I didn't steal it because if I did, I would be gone right now." He stands, reaches across the table, and palms Micah's head. "I swear on the head of Micah Yoder."

Sammi smirks.

"I'd still work here," Micah says. "I like it."

Gabe makes a frustrated sound and drops back into his seat. "Of course you do. But believe me, I'm only here because I have to be."

"I'd still be here, too." Sammi sighs. "Ten K would be nice, but it doesn't get you far in California."

"What's in California?" I ask.

"Anything," she says. "Anything that isn't this boring-ass town. The sun, for starters. Doesn't have to be California, even. I don't care."

Gabe nods slowly.

I look at Tyson. "What would you do with the money?" From driving him home, I know he doesn't exactly live in the wealthiest area.

"College," he says without hesitation. "It's all for college."

I smile. "Me too. Do you know where you want to go?"

"State," he says. "I want to be a veterinarian."

My heart melts. As if he's not already near perfect. "That's amazing!" More words threaten to bubble out of me, but for once I manage to control myself.

"Companion, Food, or Exotic?" Micah asks, which earns him more than one strange look.

"Dogs and cats, I guess." Tyson looks embarrassed. "What is that? Pets?"

"Companion," Micah says.

"I'm guessing you're going to go to some kind of genius school?" Gabe asks him. "Harvard or something?"

"Probably something more like MIT or CalTech," Micah says. "I like the hard sciences a lot."

"I'm shocked," Gabe says dryly.

"Not me," I say. "I'd rather read a book than do math. Any day."

"What about you, Zaina?" Gabe asks.

She shakes her head slightly. "I don't know. I suppose I'll find something I like in college."

"So you're going?"

"My dad wants me to," she says, then looks down with a slight laugh. "It's unlike him. So modern."

"You don't want to go?" asks Micah.

"No, I do." She bites her lip. "I'm not sure what I want to study, though."

"Why should you know?" Sammi asks. "The whole thing is ridiculous. They expect us to decide what we're going to do for the rest of our lives while we're still in high school. How do you know what you want to do when you don't know what's out there? I don't even get why they expect us to go to college right away. Wouldn't it make more sense to wait until you know what you want to do?"

"But I do want to go," Zaina says firmly, making eye contact with Sammi. "For the same reason I wanted a job." Her voice softens to its usual level. "I don't work for the money—"

Tyson winces.

"—I work because I want to show my dad I can be independent without disappointing him."

"Really?" I ask.

"Yes. My parents—my father, really—didn't want me to get a job. He doesn't think it's proper for his daughters to work. None of his sisters worked when they were growing up in Lebanon."

"Ohhh, that's where you're from!" Micah looks like he's just gotten an annoying splinter out after hours of fussing at it.

Zaina's beautiful, full mouth flattens into a line. "I've lived here since I was five years old. I'm American."

"Right, right." Micah dismisses that. "I've just always wondered. You don't have much accent to go by."

"I don't have an accent at all!" she protests.

I want to laugh, but I don't want to be the only one. I cover my mouth with one hand and look at Tyson, who is smiling a lazy smile. Sammi's face says it all, though. She has one of her dark eyebrows raised, and a smirk of disbelief.

"Z, I hate to break it to you, but you've got an accent."

"I do?" Zaina looks stunned.

We all make general noises of agreement.

"I had it narrowed down to the Middle East, but I couldn't figure out exactly what dialect," Micah says. "I even watched videos on YouTube to try to pin it down. It must be because you've lived here so long."

Zaina stares at him. "You did that?"

"I was curious."

She looks somewhere between horrified and flattered.

"It's not very noticeable," I add. It's really not.

"But yeah," Tyson says. "It's there. Don't worry, it's kinda hot."

My heart bottoms out. Tyson thinks Zaina is hot. Heat creeps up the back of my neck. Of course he does. Why wouldn't he?

"Oh." She presses her fingers to her lips.

No one says anything for a minute.

"You're all staring at me!" she protests. "You're making me self-conscious."

I flick my eyes to the nearest non-Zaina thing I can find, landing on the clock. Time is passing more quickly than I thought. I do a quick calculation to figure out how long it's been since my watch alarmed for my scheduled blood-sugar check.

I can live without knowing my blood sugar, but I'm going to need some food soon to make sure it doesn't get too low. A quick inventory of my body assures me that I'm still in a safe zone, but that doesn't mean I can wait much longer. If we can't figure out a way out of this mess, it's entirely possible I'll end up having to take my shirt off to get to my insulin pump, and that's definitely not on my to-do list for the day. Or any day.

Zaina gets a "kinda hot" accent, and I get diabetes. In a movie, she'd be the hot foreign-exchange student and I'd be, like, the friend of the geek the popular guys make a bet over.

TEN MOVIES THAT MAKE ME WISH MY LIFE WAS MORE
LIKE A MOVIE

1. Ferris Bueller's Day Off
2. 10 Things I Hate About You
3. Nick and Norah's Infinite Playlist
4. Pitch Perfect
5. The Princess Diaries
6. The Breakfast Club
7. Clueless
8. Sixteen Candles
9. Bring It On
10. Easy A

The sound of someone keying the code into the main door makes everyone jump. I didn't think anyone was still in the store besides the six of us and Mr. Solomon, and he's been in the Manager's Office since the store closed. Then it opens and Kris comes in.

"Hey, guys," he says. He's got a small stack of papers in his hand, and it occurs to me that he probably had manager-type stuff to do after close.

"You're still here?" Gabe echoes my thoughts.

"Duty calls." He flaps the papers at us as he crosses the Break Room to tap once on the door to the Manager's Office. He disappears into the office for a few minutes, and when he comes back, he's got a big grin on his face.

"Guess what, Younglings!" He claps his hands together once. "You are now my minions."

"I thought we already were," Tyson says.

"All right, you are now my . . . servants. Come on." He sweeps his arm toward the door, expecting us to get up and follow. Only Micah stands.

"What are we supposed to do?" Gabe asks.

"You're going to help clean the store! Won't that be fun?"

Everyone but Micah groans.

"Didn't Agnes already disinfect the entire place before she left?" Sammi asks.

Gabe shakes his head. "She doesn't leave, remember?

She sleeps in a freezer case."

Sammi snorts.

"Come on, my young ones." Kris coaxes us from the door with wiggly fingers. "Would you seriously rather sit in this room?"

"Than clean?" Gabe says. "Yes."

"Well, too bad. On your feet. You've got work to do."

Slowly, we follow Kris out the door. Though I'd never admit it to him, it does feel good to stand up and move around a little bit. And I'd rather have something to do to pass the time.

The late crew is still here, as it turns out, using the big motorized cleaners on the floors.

"What do you want us to do?" Micah asks.

Kris points to a large gray janitor's cart near the Self Checkouts. "There's glass cleaner and paper towels there. Find something glass and clean it."

Sammi gives him a look of disbelief. "Do you want to be more specific?"

"There's a lot of glass in here, Sammi. I don't really care what you clean." Beneath the smile, he looks tired. Really tired.

Micah is the first to act, of course, taking the cart by the wide handle and angling it toward the Bakery/Deli part of the store. I look at Tyson, and he shrugs once before following Micah. I follow him, and the others fall in behind me.

The lighting in the store is weird after-hours. There are still some low-wattage bulbs on, but not as many as there are during the day. And the back rooms behind Bakery and Deli are dark. I didn't realize how much light comes out of the circular windows at the top of the swinging doors. Without it, the display cases have a distinctly creepy look. Especially the wrapped lumps of unsliced meat in the Deli section. My mind goes to horror-movie places.

I'm not the only one, either. "Shh," Gabe says, and everyone stills. "If you listen closely, you can hear the butchers grinding up human flesh for the sausages." Then he lets loose with an evil laugh.

"You have got to be the most immature idiot I've ever met," Sammi says, giving him a shove.

"Says the girl who just hit me." He rubs his shoulder theatrically.

"Where should we start?" Micah asks. He's holding a spray bottle and a handful of paper towels, and looking back and forth between the Deli and Bakery.

"I call Bakery," Sammi says, crossing over to the less horror-movie-set side of the aisle. At night, the bakery cases are just plain empty. Only a few crumbs on the very bottom shelves indicate that there used to be cakes, cookies, and rolls in there.

We split into small groups and work the area together. Now that the overhead Christmas music is gone, I can hear the hum of the refrigeration units below as I polish the glass in front of the empty platters where deli salads and prepared foods were during the day. I can also hear the steady whir and whoosh of the floor polisher a few aisles away. Somewhere, someone is listening to a portable radio, but it's too far to make out the song.

Zaina is scrubbing the case beside me. It's funny how even though I'm being quiet, too, I can't stop fixating on how long it's been since she spoke. She hasn't said a word since we started cleaning. The silence is starting to feel like a giant bubble between us, pushing us apart and drowning out any noise either of us might make.

So, when she speaks, I nearly jump out of my skin, and she apologizes: "Sorry, I didn't mean to startle you."

"No, it's fine. I was lost in thought, I guess. What did you say?"

"I said I hate cleaning windows." She makes a face.

I can't help smiling. "I'd rather do windows than floors."

"I wouldn't mind the floors if I could ride on that machine." Her hazel eyes light up.

Laughter bursts out of me at the image of Zaina riding the big industrial floor cleaner. It's like a miniature Zamboni. She would look ridiculous up there, but I love the idea. "I've always wanted to ride one of those scooter carts we have up front," I confess.

Gabe overhears us. "Which one do you think would win in a race?"

"Forget that, I just want to bring my board in here." Sammi rocks back into a skateboarding stance. "I could totally grind the cases over in meats."

"That would be epic," Gabe agrees.

"I've always wanted to ride my bike in the store," Micah adds. "You know, when it's empty in the morning? Did you ever want to do that as a kid? Like at Target or Walmart, when they have the big bike section and you can try them out?"

"Totally," Sammi says. "I used to do laps around the bike section, and my parents would be all, 'Samantha, stop that! You're going to hurt someone!'" She scolds herself in the strangled whisper of a parent trying not to draw attention to an out-of-control kid.

"I was a runner," Gabe says. "My parents used to keep me on one of those leashes."

"What?" Zaina's expression is priceless.

"It's supposed to look like a fuzzy backpack, but it's a leash." Gabe mimes trying to make a break for it and getting yanked back on the end of an invisible line.

Tyson laughs. "Somebody ought to leash you now."

"I remember the first time I went to a hotel," I say. "When the elevator doors opened, and I saw that long hall"—I can still picture it in my mind and my pulse accelerates—"I just took off."

"There's something about big empty spaces," Gabe agrees, gesturing around us at the wide aisles.

"Let's have a race," Sammi says, tossing her wad of paper towels to the ground.

I laugh, but then I see she's serious. "We can't do that."

"Why not?" she asks.

"Because we're already in trouble," I say.

She rolls her eyes. "(A) Exactly my point. What else are they going to do to us? And (B) We didn't do anything wrong. Besides, who says a race is wrong? They probably won't even notice. We'll be back before anyone figures it out."

"I don't want to lose my job," Micah says.

"Me neither," Tyson agrees.

"Fine." Sammi hunkers down and tightens the laces on her Vans. "You don't have to race. Gabe, you in?"

He tosses his paper towels over his shoulder. "I'm so in."

"Anyone else?" Sammi asks. "No?" She goes into a sprinter's stance and Gabe lines up beside her.

"Me!" Zaina blurts out, and Sammi almost falls out of her pose.

She recovers quickly, though, shooting a grin at Zaina. "Hell yeah! Let's do this."

"Me too," I say. I set my spray bottle and towels on top of the Deli case, then I line up with my toes against the edge of the same floor tile as the others.

"On your marks," Sammi intones, "get set . . . GO!"

Gabe is off the line before anyone else, and I know in that instant that no one is going to beat him. Still, I run as fast as I can. My Converse make slapping sounds on the hard floor as I rush past the end of the Deli section and take a left through Seafood.

Sammi passes me on my left, making up ground on Gabe, but not getting close enough to overtake him. Zaina is keeping pace with me to my right. We separate as we enter Meats, and the huge refrigerated bunkers block the center of the aisle. Down the wine aisle, I get a glimpse of the big ride-on floor cleaner, but then it's gone.

Behind me I hear the sound of pounding feet and I glance over my shoulder to see Tyson and Micah bearing down on me with wicked speed. I veer right as the meat bunkers end, and then Zaina and I are approaching the glass dairy cases together while both Micah and Tyson whiz by us.

My lungs burn by the time we pass the yogurt, but I only slow my pace a little. It's not far until the left turn into Frozen Foods. The others are already out of sight. I can't remember the last time I ran this hard. I can barely remember the last time I ran. My doctor got me excused from gym for the last three years because my blood sugar would get too low during class. I may have exaggerated a bit to stay out this year, so I haven't been running in a long, long time.

Zaina passes me in the ice-cream section, but I don't care. When I round the turn to see all the quiet registers, the others are so far ahead that they're almost to Floral. From there, they only have to make it through Produce and they'll be back to the starting point.

Still I run. From up ahead I hear laughter, and then Gabe's voice. "Bet those cigarettes don't sound like such a good idea now, huh, Samantha?"

"Fuck . . . you," Sammi pants.

The others are slowing a bit through Produce. All the display cases are set at angles here, making a straight line through the department impossible. I've managed to cut some of their lead by the time I run past the empty case where they put out the fresh-cut fruit every morning. But it's no contest—I'm going to be dead last. A stitch in my side takes the last of my speed, and I have to walk the final ten yards or so with the heel of my hand bracing my ribs.

"Woo-hoo! She made it!" Gabe cheers when I cross the finish line.

I lean forward and gasp for breath. My heart is pounding. "Who . . . won?"

"Me!" Gabe crows. "Take that, suckers!"

"You had a head start and you barely beat me," Tyson says.

"Your hesitation cost you, man," Gabe says.

I try to straighten up, but the world goes gray when I do, so I slump back down to hold myself up on my knees. I'm breathing embarrassingly hard. Without getting up again, I look toward the Produce section. There's no sign that anyone has followed us. I can't believe we got away with a race through the store. I laugh a wheezy, out-of-breath laugh.

"Little out of shape there, hey, Red?" Sammi pants at me, whacking me on the back.

"You don't sound so great yourself," Tyson says.

"Still came in third," she says.

On my second attempt to straighten up, I manage it. My chest is still heaving, but at least I'm upright. I check out the others, but they don't look nearly as bad as me. Not even Zaina, who was almost as slow as I was. Her cheeks are pink, and she's breathing a little heavier than usual, but that's it.

At least the boys have the grace to be sweaty. Gabe is hopping from foot to foot like a cartoon rabbit. "That was fun. Let's go again!" he says with a grin.

Sammi flaps a hand at him. "God, no. I need a cigarette."

"I need . . . some water," I gasp.

"Aisle three," Sammi says.

"Ha-ha," I pant.

"I've got a bottle back in the Break Room," Micah volunteers. "Do you want me to go get it?"

I nod and go back to hands-on-knees. "Yes . . . please."

I'm going to need more than water soon; I know it. My fingers are still tingling, even though I've caught my breath. For the first time all day, I pray for the police to come quickly.

## THINGS I HAVE LEARNED DURING THIS SHIFT

1. Sammi is not as evil as advertised.
2. Zaina is Lebanese.
3. I cannot be trusted to gather carts from the parking lot.
4. There is a lot more glass in a grocery store than I ever realized.
5. I never want to become a janitor, high-rise window washer, or a manager at GoodFoods Market.
6. My mother actually does have untapped reservoirs of guilt saved up for special occasions like today.
7. It is possible to look forward to being questioned by the police.

"Do you think the cops are really on their way?" Zaina pauses with the door to the eggs propped open in her left hand. Cold air pours out in rolling waves around her knees and feet, and every circle she cleared in the condensation with her paper towels is already fogging over.

"What do you mean?" I ask. I'm two doors down in front of the skim milk, polishing away at the outside of the glass.

"We've been waiting an awfully long time," she says. "I wonder if they're actually coming."

"Do you think he'd lie about calling?" Tyson wonders from the sour-cream-and-cottage-cheese cooler.

"I don't know what to think," Zaina says. She's been much more talkative since the race. "I just can't believe how long we've been waiting."

It's true. We've already worked our way from Bakery and Deli, through Seafood and Meat to the Dairy section. The only glass left is Frozen Foods. Admittedly, that's still a pretty major job, but it does make you wonder what's taking so long.

My stomach growls.

"You think Solomon's trying to trick us?" Sammi asks.

"I don't think he would lie." Micah's voice is muffled from inside the whole-milk section.

"Who knows." Tyson sighs.

"Can they even talk to us without our parents here?" I

ask. "If they are on their way, I mean."

"They can talk to me," Gabe reminds us. "I'm eighteen."

"Gee, really, Gabe? That's the first I'm hearing of this," Sammi says with an eye roll.

Micah emerges from behind his door. "I think they can interview us as witnesses, even if our parents don't give permission."

I make a mental note to look up the rules on this kind of stuff. Seems like the sort of knowledge that might come in handy. Not that I'm planning to have a lot of face time with the police, but still.

Bending to polish the lowest corners of the glass doors makes my head swim, but not as badly as straightening up again. I press a palm to the door to steady myself, leaving a print on the glass I've just cleaned.

Great.

Out of nowhere, Sammi turns and does a jump shot to sink her used-up paper towels into the open garbage at the end of the janitor's cart we're still trailing. "I think I'm going to go," she says.

"Go where?" Gabe asks.

"Just . . . go." She swipes her hand into an unseen distance.

"You can't," Micah says.

"What are they going to do?" she asks. "*Kris* is going to chase me down and put me under citizen's arrest? Yeah, right."

"Sammi, you can't just leave," Tyson says.

She raises both eyebrows at him and takes two steps backward, then turns and heads for the front of the store. "See ya!" she calls over her shoulder.

The rest of us turn into statues, unsure what to do. I can't even make myself look at anyone else—my eyes are glued to her short form as she saunters down one of the ethnic-food aisles. Then she's past the prepackaged curries and out of sight. Her shoes are too quiet to make any sound on the floor. Still, I watch, expecting her to come right back, escorted by one of the bosses.

"Do you really think she's going to leave?" Micah asks.

"Sammi likes to talk tough, but I don't think she'd actually do anything," Gabe says, though he sounds uncertain.

No one moves for a long, quiet moment. Finally, I speak up. "I'll go check on her." Mostly I need to satisfy the small ball of panic that's starting to gain speed in my chest. I hate the idea that she might be defying Kris and Mr. Solomon. I've always been the kind of kid who could be counted on to watch the class if the teacher had to step out.

"You don't even know where she went," Tyson says.

The panic ball doesn't care about reason. The panic ball needs to be soothed. "I'll check the Break Room."

Unexpectedly, Zaina steps forward. "I'll come with you."

"Um . . . okay." I head for the aisle we last saw her. When I've got a clear view of it, it's obvious she's not just hiding out of sight to scare us.

Zaina walks beside me, but she doesn't say anything until we get to the front of the store. "Do you think she really left?" she asks.

"I don't know." She would have had to be moving pretty fast to get her coat and already be out of the door without us seeing a trace of her. I bite my lip. I thought we'd have spotted her by now.

"Break Room," Zaina reminds me.

I follow her, but before we reach it, the door opens and Kris comes out.

"What are you doing?" he asks.

"I have to go to the bathroom." The lie springs to my lips without thought.

"Me too." Zaina's voice is barely a whisper.

"Then why are you coming in here?" he asks.

My nerves crackle, but I tell him another lie. "Girl stuff."

He looks away. Girl stuff is kryptonite to the male of the species. "All right, but make it quick," he says.

We go into the Break Room for a moment, because we don't have a choice.

Inside, Zaina whispers, "How long do we have to stand here?"

I shrug and my stomach growls again. For the first time, it occurs to me that someone must have thrown away the rest of my lunch when I went into the office to talk with Mr. Solomon. It had been gone when I came out. So was my book, for that matter.

My money's on Agnes, the cleaning machine. But what would she have done with my book? I scan the room, noticing the cookie trays and the nasty eggnog carton are gone, too. There's nothing to eat in here; I don't know why I'm rechecking.

"Okay, let's go." Zaina interrupts my thoughts.

Kris is sitting cross-legged on one of the bagging conveyors when we come out. Just sitting on it, like he's waiting to be bagged and taken home for someone's dinner. He straightens up when he sees us, seeming to come out of a trance, but he doesn't say anything.

Now, of course, we're stuck going to the bathroom. He's watching our every move. So much for my great cover story.

We walk quickly to the ladies' room, though I scan as much of the store as I can see for any trace of Sammi. Nothing. When Zaina opens the door, the motion-sensor lights are already on, still blue in their warm-up phase, making the bathroom look like it's underwater. The room is shockingly cold. I knew they turned the heat down in the store after closing, but it feels like I've taken a wrong turn into one of the freezer cases. I shiver involuntarily.

"Who's there?" Sammi's voice echoes from one of the stalls.

"It's me. Chloe. And Zaina's with me."

"What are you doing here?" she asks.

"Thought you were leaving," I challenge.

"No," she drawls. "I said I had to *go*. To the bathroom."

"Well, we had to pee, too," I say, though I don't.

"Excuse me." Zaina ducks her head as she walks past me, heading for a stall.

A toilet flushes and Sammi emerges, her regulation uniform shirt now draped over one arm, exposing the T-shirt she was wearing beneath. It's got an old-fashioned telephone booth on it, only it's blue and says *POLICE* across the top. I never would have guessed she was a Whovian. She nods to me as she approaches the sink, but doesn't say anything.

"Everyone thought you left," I say, even though I want to talk about her T-shirt. I congratulate myself on my focus.

"Good."

"Why do you do stuff like that?" I ask.

"What's that supposed to mean?"

"Like, saying stuff just to get people freaked out."

She shrugs, and slings her uniform shirt around her neck like a scarf. "Why be boring?"

"Can't you be interesting without being mean?"

"It's not mean. Don't be such a Boy Scout."

Ouch. Okay, so I obviously wasn't a Boy Scout, but I definitely stayed in Girl Scouts longer than most of the girls in my class. Earned some serious badges. I didn't have the guts to tell my mom I didn't want to do it anymore. Not like that's news. I've never even had the guts to tell her I hate it that she comes into the doctor's office with me.

Today is the first time in a long time that I can actually remember breaking rules on purpose. Not to mention covering up the accident in the parking lot. I lied to my own mother about why I'm still stuck at work. I'm even standing up to Sammi.

Well, a little anyway.

"I'm not a Boy Scout," I say softly.

Sammi laughs her *heh!* laugh. "Right." She finishes washing her hands and leans across the counter to inspect her bangs.

"Is that your natural color?" I ask.

"Nope. Is that yours?"

"Yeah." I look at my own reflection, not surprised to see that my ponytail has slumped a bit to one side and I've got a corona of escaped curls all around my face. Not the pretty, romantic kind, just the frizzy half and three-quarter circles that come from having curly hair get wet and then dry.

"It's a pretty badass color," Sammi says unexpectedly.

I meet her eyes in the mirror again, startled. "Really?"

"Yeah." She sounds surprised at my skeptical tone. "Red is definitely cool. You should get some bright red or blue highlights or something. Then you'd be a total badass."

"My mom won't let me," I say automatically. I know it for a fact. I've always wanted to color my hair. Make it anything but this, but she says it would be a shame to cover up natural red.

"She'd get over it," Sammi says. "It's not that big a deal.

I mean, hell, GoodFoods carries a couple brands of the punk colors. How hard-core can it be?"

"Really?" I've never noticed them before. Then again, I don't spend a lot of time looking at the hair-dye section of the store. There's never been a point. "Is it hard to do?"

I can't believe I'm having this conversation.

"Nah. It's kind of messy, but it's easy."

We hear a soft cough from the stalls, and I realize Zaina's still in there.

"Zaina? Are you okay?"

"Can you please wait outside or something?" she calls. "I can't go with you listening."

"Stage fright?" Sammi hollers. "Can't pee when we're talking to you?"

"Please," Zaina begs.

"Aww, don't be so shy." Sammi laughs.

I giggle, but wave a hand at Sammi. "Don't tease her."

"Just relax and think of Niagara Falls, Z!" she shouts.

"Sammi!" I whisper, but I'm laughing, too.

"Could you please leave me alone?" Zaina's voice is desperate.

"Oh, fine." Sammi throws her head back and starts to sing, "The sun'll come out tomorrow!"

I join her, tentatively at first, but my voice gets stronger when I realize Sammi has no intention of quitting before the big finish. Soon we're both belting, "To-morrow! To-morrow! I love ya! To-morrow!" at the top of our lungs.

Someone pounds on the door, hard enough to make it waft open an inch. "What's going on in there?" It's Solomon's voice.

I put my foot on the door, shoving it closed. "Nothing! Girl stuff!" My heart pounds. I can't believe I said that to the big boss.

Sammi laughs and adds, "Tampons!" in a piping voice.

"Well, hurry it up. This is not playtime."

*This is not playtime,* Sammi mouths with a stern finger pointed at me.

I cover my mouth to smother laughter.

"Do you hear me?" Solomon shouts.

I uncover long enough to shout, "Loud and clear!" before slapping my hand back over my mouth.

The stall door opens and Zaina peeks out, looking pale. "He didn't come in, did he?"

"No." Sammi shakes her head. "Chloe ninja-kicked the door shut." She strikes a pose, hands raised in karate readiness.

Zaina ducks her head and goes to the sink to wash her hands. She hisses when she touches the water. "So cold!"

"Seriously."

I tuck my fingers under my arms. "I'm not even sure I *could* pee at this temperature."

"You may change your mind if they keep us here much longer."

"Speaking of that—" Sammi waves me aside and flings the door open, but no one is outside anymore. "You can't hold us here against our wills, you know!" she shouts into the void. "This is kidnapping!"

Zaina gasps and flattens herself against the wall beside the hand dryer. I stand on my toes behind Sammi, looking over her shoulder for Solomon and Kris. "Who are you talking to?" I ask.

"Trust me, they hear." She raises her voice back to shouting level. "Kidnapping!"

"We're already in trouble, Sammi." I might be a little more badass than usual today, but there are limits. "Maybe you shouldn't antagonize Mr. Solomon right now."

"Whatever. They've obviously decided we're a bunch of criminals." Sammi slips her arms through Zaina's and mine and leads the way to the Frozen Foods section. "Come on. The boys should have finished up in Dairy by now, don't you think?"

She's right. They've rounded the corner at the far end of Frozen Foods, causing the motion sensors in the cases to illuminate them like beacons while the rest of the aisle is dark. That changes as we walk toward them, the bulbs reacting to our approach by flicking to life. It's like we're creating our own runway lights.

Gabe, who is working on the lower half of the door in front of Juice, looks up, then stands suddenly when he sees Sammi. "I thought you left."

"Just need a little break," she says. "You know how it is."

"I thought—" he starts again, and then cuts himself off. "Never mind."

"It's freezing over here!" Zaina hugs herself.

"That's kind of the point." Tyson smiles at her.

"But does it have to be so cold?"

"Yes," Micah answers.

"I never thought I'd say this, but I wish the cops would hurry up and get here," Gabe says. "I'm so done with cleaning."

"You'd seriously rather be arrested than stuck here cleaning?" Tyson asks.

"I'm not going to be arrested." Gabe sounds completely confident.

I spray down the door in front of a display of ice-cream sandwiches and my stomach growls again.

"Chloe, are you okay?" Tyson asks. "You look kind of pale."

I find a smile and try not to make direct eye contact when I answer with a breezy, "Fine!" and then change the subject. "You guys, seriously, who do you think would have done this?"

"Agnes," Sammi says without hesitation.

Everyone reacts with the same kind of shock I feel.

"Why her?" Tyson asks.

Sammi turns, propping one hand on her hip. "Seriously, it's the perfect cover. She seems like the model employee. She's worked here forever. She's probably got, like, a million cats at home and she needs more money for Cat Chow."

Gabe laughs. "Maybe she's been secretly embezzling from the company all this time, and one day she's not going to show up for work and we'll find out she fled the country."

"To live on a private island with all her cats," Sammi adds.

"I'm serious, you guys."

"Oh, come on, Chloe. We'll never figure this out. It could have been anybody. It could have been Solomon himself."

"There's got to be something we're missing. Some clue. I checked out the padlock earlier, but there were no marks—" I cut myself off with a gasp. "Oh my God."

"What?" Micah asks.

I drop to a crouch and brace my head with my hands. "I'm so stupid!"

"Did you figure it out?" Tyson asks.

"No!" I look up at them. "I touched the padlock earlier. My fingerprints are going to be all over it. They're going to think it was me!"

"No, no." Tyson hunkers down in front of me and puts a hand on my arm. "I'm sure there are tons of fingerprints on the box. Don't worry about it."

"How could I be so stupid?" I squeeze my eyes shut. "I'm not a detective. What was I thinking?"

"So, wait. You've actually been trying to solve this? Like a detective?" Sammi's voice is closer than I expected, and I open my eyes to find them all in a loose circle around me. Tyson is still down on my level.

Heat rushes into my face for the kajillionth time, but I don't fight it. What's the point? I've already embarrassed myself enough today. "Yes," I admit. "I don't know. I was bored, I guess, and it was at least something kind of interesting to think about. I thought maybe I could—never mind." Not that I'd be willing to admit it out loud, but I kind of loved the idea of being the one to solve it before the cops got here. Too much Nancy Drew in my past, too much Sherlock Holmes in my present.

"I can't picture you in police academy," Gabe says thoughtfully.

The flush in my cheeks deepens. "I don't want to be a cop." I feel like a dork. "I read too many mysteries, I guess. It's stupid, I know."

"It's not stupid," Micah says. He's now sitting cross-legged, facing me from a short distance away. "Who says you can't solve a mystery? Maybe you'll be a detective later."

"Seriously?" I look at him in disbelief. Who goes around planning to be a detective? But that makes me wonder about him. "What do you want to do?" I ask.

"Ideally, I'd like to be on the first manned flight to Mars, but I don't know if I'll qualify." The look on his face says he's dead serious. "If not, I still want to work for NASA. I think it would be almost as good to be on the team on Earth for the Mars flight."

No one says anything for a few beats. Surprisingly, it's Zaina who speaks first. "I believe you will, Micah."

He smiles widely. "Thank you, Zaina."

Sammi nudges Gabe's foot with hers. "What are you going to do next year?"

He sighs as he leans back against the frozen-veggies case. "College. Basketball. Same shit, different school."

"Do you even like basketball?"

He shrugs. "I don't *not* like it. It's just that I don't really have a choice so it's hard to care."

"Why don't you have a choice?" Micah asks.

"My dad went to Notre Dame. My brother and sister both went to Notre Dame. I'm a *legacy*. That's where I'm going."

"You don't get any say? That's kind of rough." I shift to sit since my legs are starting to fall asleep. It's numbingly cold on the floor with my back against the freezer, but I don't want to move right now. I wrap my arms around my upraised knees.

"That's kind of bullshit," Sammi says.

Gabe nods, but he looks down at the ground. "I wish he'd let me have some input in *where* I was going to go."

"Why don't you apply to some other places?" I ask.

"He'll only pay if I go to Notre Dame."

"Good problems to have," Tyson says.

He's been quiet, and now we all look at him.

He licks his lips. "College is a given for you. I have to work my butt off just to get there."

Gabe's mouth moves like he's trying to say something, but he can't work it out.

"So, you know, just be glad you know you're going," Tyson adds.

"Dude, I get it." Gabe puts his hands up. "Poor little rich kid whining about how hard his life is. That's why I didn't bring it up."

"Where would you go if you had a choice?" I ask.

"Honestly? I don't even know. I've never really thought about it since it wasn't an option."

"It *is* an option," Tyson insists.

"Not if I want my dad to be happy."

"Who cares if he's happy?" Sammi asks.

Gabe stares at her for a long moment. "I guess I do."

"What about what you want?"

He shrugs. "It's a good school."

"That's not the point."

"Sometimes it's easier to go along with what makes other people happy."

"Oh, really?" Sammi looks at him, and I have a feeling she's not just talking about school.

"I understand," Zaina speaks up. "My dad expects me to be a certain way, and most of the time, it's easier to cooperate."

"How does he feel about you not wearing the *hijab*?" Micah uses both forefingers to trace the outline of a head scarf.

"He doesn't mind that so much. My mother doesn't wear it, either." She shrugs. "But other things . . . sometimes it's not worth the fight."

"I know the feeling." Micah nods.

"What's your deal, anyway?" Sammi asks. "Why are you homeschooled?" She says the last word like it tastes bad.

"I started out in regular school. For kindergarten, you know? But it was too easy. My parents wanted me to move up to first grade, but the school wouldn't let me because I was too young. So my parents decided to homeschool me for kindergarten, and then first grade. They thought maybe the rest of the class would catch up and then I could go to school."

"Did you?" I ask.

He shakes his head. "See, I'm really smart." And because it's Micah talking, no one protests. I don't even think he's trying to brag.

He continues, "I just kept getting further and further ahead of people my age, so there was never a time I could go back in. So, I stayed out. My sister, too."

"Does it get boring?" I ask.

"Not really. We do a lot of stuff outside the house, depending on what we're studying. But honestly, that's why I wanted to get a job," Micah says. "I have other homeschool friends, and some friends in my neighborhood. Sometimes I do video chats with my teachers or other homeschoolers, but it's not the same as being in the same room with other people. Do you know what I mean?"

"Believe me, it's overrated." Sammi crosses her arms.

"I don't understand."

"Haven't you heard? 'Hell is other people.'"

"Jean-Paul Sartre," Micah says.

She rolls her eyes. "You do know everything."

"Don't you think that's a little cliché?" I ask. "The whole high-school-is-hell thing? I mean, it's not great, but it's not horrible every minute, right?"

"You should try it being me," Sammi says.

"What's so bad about being you?" Tyson asks. His tone says she's full of it.

"Gosh, where should I start?" She clasps her hands with mock enthusiasm. "Well, there's getting called a dyke every day. There's the fact that none of the girls will talk to me because they think I'm checking them out, and none of the guys will talk to me because they think I'm into girls."

"Are you?" Micah asks.

She gives him a look. "Are you serious?"

He nods. "I don't know what you are. How would I know if I didn't ask?"

Her pale mouth hardens into a line. "No. I'm not. I like guys, okay?"

"Huh," Tyson says in surprise. I check the others for their reactions. Zaina is watching Sammi intently, Gabe seems distracted by something on his pants, and Micah is nodding.

I can't be the only one wondering. "Then why do you dress like that?" I ask.

Sammi looks down at her baggy jeans and skater shoes. "I like my clothes. Why do you dress the way you do?"

"Me?" My clothes are about as middle-of-the-road as you can get. I don't like to stand out. Red hair has always done that for me without any extra help.

"Yeah. Why do you have purple shoes? Why do you wear glasses? Why do you always have your hair in a pony-tail?"

"I—I don't know. I just do."

"Exactly. I dress the way I feel like I should dress." Sammi runs a hand over her short blond hair. "If people are so narrow-minded that they think I'm gay just because I have short hair, that's not my problem."

"But if it makes you miserable at school, why wouldn't you try to fit in more?" I ask.

"Because that makes me miserable, too. Why should I have to fit in with everyone else's idea of what makes someone beautiful? Why does everyone care so much? I'll never look as good as Zaina, so what's the point?"

Zaina startles at the mention of her name. "You don't want to be beautiful," she says.

"Everyone wants to be beautiful." My eyes roam over the black waterfall of hair swept over her shoulder.

"People make assumptions about me, too," she says.

"Because you're Muslim?" Micah asks.

"Most people don't know that I am," she says. "They think because I don't wear the *hijab* that I'm something else. Greek, Russian, Mexican . . . whatever they want me to be."

"Does that bother you?" I ask.

"Not really."

"So, what did you mean about assumptions?" Tyson asks.

"They assume that because I'm beautiful, that I'm cold. And mean." She looks down, her lashes brushing her cheeks. "And that I'm easy."

"What?" Sammi asks.

"People assume that beautiful girls are sluts," she says.

"Bullshit," Sammi says.

Gabe sucks air through his teeth. "I think she's kind of right."

"You think just because a girl is pretty that she wants to screw everyone?" Sammi demands.

"A lot of guys do," he says. Fire lights in Sammi's eyes, and Gabe searches the rest of us for backup. "Tyson, help me out. Don't you think that's true?"

"I don't know." Tyson looks uncomfortable. "*I* don't think that, but maybe other guys do. I don't know."

Gabe settles on me next. "Chloe. Be honest. Who's the most beautiful girl at your school?"

It's an easy question. "Jessica Mueller."

"And what do you think of her?"

I picture Jessica in my head. Tall; long, sleek brown hair; perfect skin. She's probably the most popular girl in school. Hangs out with all the coolest guys. Rumor has it she's been with at least half of them. And that's just what I've heard as the new kid. It's not like people spend a lot of time talking to me. I lick my lips. "They say she's kind of a slut, I guess."

Sammi sighs. "High school is complete bullshit."

"I don't know if she is, though," I try. "I'm new."

Zaina pushes the bulk of her hair behind her shoulders. "See? I'm right."

My ears go hot again. "Maybe."

"People at my school assume the same thing about me," Zaina says.

"And are you? A slut, I mean?" Gabe asks her.

She glares at him. "No. Are you?"

"It doesn't work like that." He grins, showing off his dimples. "I mean, I've been with some girls, but that doesn't make me a slut."

"And being with some guys doesn't make Jessica Mueller a slut, either," Sammi says, shooting me a dirty look.

The heat in my ears spreads across my temples and cheeks. "I know that."

"So, you see? People make assumptions about you no matter what you look like," Zaina concludes.

"Amen to that." Tyson holds his hand up for a fist bump. Zaina looks at it curiously for a second, then bumps, smiling. "You should try going into a store looking like me," he says. "Everyone thinks I'm there to rob it."

Of course the chatterbox center in my brain has something to add. "When I go into a store at the mall, someone always follows me because middle-class white girls are the biggest shoplifters."

Tyson laughs. "Seriously?"

I nod, and so does Sammi. "I know it's not the same thing, but . . ."

"That's funny," he says. "It's not as bad as people crossing the street when they see you coming, but I feel you." He leans into me for a moment, our shoulders touching.

"People don't bother crossing the street when they see me coming," Sammi says with a grin. "They'd rather be up close when they call me names."

Considering we're talking about racism and harassment, I can't quite figure out why we're all smiling. Maybe it's just the fact that we're all on the same page about something. Or maybe you just have to laugh at horrible things sometimes.

Zaina sighs. "Most people are kind, though. Don't you think? The bad ones just stick in your mind so much longer."

"I think that's true for everyone," Gabe says. "No matter who you are. When people are shitty to you, it can really mess you up."

"Even if those people are your dad?" Sammi asks with an eyebrow raised. And just like that, the good humor drains from the group. Gabe holds her gaze, both of them still, like big cats facing off in the jungle.

Finally Gabe speaks, and his words sound a lot more casual than his tone. "Easy there. I think we've had enough warm fuzziness for now."

Part of my brain had taken in the fact that the riding floor-scrubber sounds were getting closer, but it's still something of a surprise when the night-crew guy rounds the end of the aisle on board the big gray machine. He looks just as startled to find us sitting on the floor in the Freezer section.

"Guess we're done here," Tyson says, rising to his feet.

"Thank God." Gabe pushes off the cooler and lopes over to the janitorial cart to give it a shove toward the far end of the aisle.

Tyson extends a hand to Zaina, helping her to her feet, then does the same for me. I can't tamp down the little thrill in my skin when he touches me. I whisper a thank-you and tuck my hands into my apron pockets as soon as I've got my balance. Never mind the fact that my head is swimming from the position change.

"Now what should we clean?" Micah asks.

"I want to know where the damn police are," Sammi says.

Gabe smirks. "I thought you were all anticop. You

weren't going to let the man get your fingerprints and all that."

"Whatever. I just want to get the hell out of here. I don't care how it happens anymore."

"Kris was up front before," I remind her. "Maybe he knows something."

"He'd better." She takes the lead, striding down the aisle faster than I would have given her credit for at her height. The rest of us trail after her, me in the rear once again.

"Are you all right?" Micah asks me, slowing his pace to let me close the gap between us.

"I'm hungry," I say. This is putting it mildly. And it's not entirely accurate. I'm so far past the point of needing to eat that I'm slightly nauseated. This is bad. I have to do something about this soon. Very, very soon. I should tell someone, but now I feel like I've pushed past the point where I can tell anyone without revealing that I was trying to hide it. Which just makes the fact that I've been hiding it that much lamer. It's a Catch-22 of idiocy.

Why can't I just do what I need to do and not worry about it? *Hear that, pancreas?* I ask. *Just do what you need to do.*

It never listens.

My stomach growls again.

Micah glances at his watch. "I'm hungry, too."

"This is taking longer than I thought."

"Are you sure you're all right?"

*No.* "I'm okay."

But he doesn't go back to his quicker pace, instead staying near me, and for that, I'm grateful.

TEN SIGNS YOUR BLOOD SUGAR IS GETTING TOO LOW, OR RAISE YOUR HAND IF YOU HAVE ALL TEN OF THESE SYMPTOMS RIGHT NOW, CHLOE, YOU IDIOT

1. Shaking
2. Sweating
3. Sleepiness
4. Blurry vision
5. Heart palpitations
6. Confusion
7. Tingling in the hands, feet, or face
8. Difficulty speaking
9. Weakness
10. Fainting

Kris is still sitting in his Zen position on the powered-down conveyor belt when we get to the front of the store.

I'm not sure if he's lost in thought, or what, but he doesn't move as we approach. And it's not like we're quiet about it.

He jumps when Gabe asks, "How much longer do we have to stay here, Kris? It's Christmas Eve, man."

"The cops should be here soon," he says. His usual cheerful tone has gone flat. "They said this is a low-priority call, though."

Gabe sighs loudly. "This sucks!"

"I still don't get why Mr. Solomon's keeping us and no one else," Tyson says.

"I don't get why Micah's here at all," Sammi says.

"It's okay," Micah says.

"But it's Christmas Eve," Gabe repeats.

"At least it's not Christmas Day."

"I'm going to miss dinner," Tyson sighs. "And my grandma's cooking."

"My mom's going to kill me," I say. "And my brother came home from college today."

"You guys, I don't want to be here, either. Can you quit bitching at me?" Kris looks at us, and we fall silent. Then he shakes his head. "Sorry. I—can you all just go to the Break Room?"

"Don't you want us to clean some more?" Micah asks, then winces when Gabe elbows him.

"No. Just go wait, okay?"

I study him as we file past to the Break Room, but I can't get any solid clues as to what's on his mind. He's definitely not himself right now. Judging from the quiet among the others, they're feeling it, too.

When we're safely behind the heavy door to the Break Room, Sammi asks, "What's up his butt?"

"I don't know," Gabe says. "But he is not happy right now."

"He probably wants to go home, like we do," Tyson says.

"Yeah . . ." Sammi looks at the door. "Maybe."

I move past them and take a seat at one of the tables. I'm so worn out from washing all the glass. Not to mention our little race.

"What are we supposed to do now?" Micah asks.

"There's nothing *to* do," Sammi says.

"Sure there is," Gabe counters.

"All right, then, what do *you* want to do?" she asks.

## THINGS GABE WANTED TO DO THAT COULDN'T BE DONE

1. Play poker. (No cards, no chips, no money.)
2. Plan a prison-style escape. (No windows, only one door, no skills that would be useful in a prison break.)

3. Eat. (Nothing in the staff refrigerator but a can of Diet Coke with someone else's name on it.)
4. Watch hilarious videos on YouTube. (Work computers block all social networking sites; cell network service is crappy in the store.)
5. Play basketball. (No basket, no ball.)

THINGS GABE WANTED TO DO THAT COULD BE DONE
1. Play Name That Tune using everyone's playlists.

"How can you not know this song?" Gabe demands, making his phone dance at Sammi. An upbeat song with a driving guitar line wails at us from its tiny speaker. "They only play it on the radio, like, five times a day."

"Which is why I don't listen to the radio," she says.

"It's like you're deliberately ignoring the culture of your own generation," he says.

"Culture?" She raises her eyebrow. "Please."

"I don't know the song, either," Micah says.

Their voices stretch like taffy in my head, making my eyes water. I look down, and the room takes a moment to catch up with me.

Oh crap.

"Try this." Sammi cranks the volume on her own

phone, trying to drown out Gabe's pop song with something more electronica. "This is music!" she shouts over the din.

"Sounds like a bunch of noise." Gabe sticks his finger in his ear, wincing.

"You're both crazy." Tyson jumps into the fray. "Neither of you know what real music sounds like."

"And I suppose you do?"

Sweat prickles my back. Experimentally, I lift my hands off my knees and feel them both jittering madly. This is so not good. I glance at my watch, but the numbers seem to dance and I can't be sure of the time. My insulin pump is still merrily dumping insulin into my bloodstream, and I don't have any food in my system to take the hit.

This is so, so, so bad.

Suddenly the painful mix of Sammi's and Gabe's songs cuts off and Tyson brings up one of his own. I think I recognize the song, but my ears won't make sense of it. Like I can't be bothered to understand the words, even though they're in English.

So. Not. Good.

I look around the spinning room. The trays of Christmas cookies I'd so carefully avoided are gone. I already know there's nothing in the refrigerator. This is nuts. It's a grocery store, for God's sake. The place is full of food. But there's nothing in the Break Room. With the store closed tomorrow, Agnes probably went on one of her cleaning sprees and tossed everything that could spoil.

I'm screwed. Shutting off my pump is the only answer, and it's not even a good answer. I have to go back to the bathroom to do it in private, and I'm pretty sure I can't make it that far. My blood sugar is tanking, fast. I can feel it with each droplet of sweat forming on my temples. Looking up, spots dance in front of my eyes.

"Does anyone have any juice?" I ask.

No one hears me over the sound of Tyson's song, and Gabe and Sammi's loud argument.

I try again, but my voice can't push much past a mumble.

Zaina notices me and tilts her head like a curious dog.

"I need juice," I say.

"What?" She leans closer.

I shake my head as best I can.

"Would you three be quiet?" she says loudly, startling the others into silence. Then she turns back to me. "What did you say?"

"I need juice," I say.

"No shit, I'm hungry, too," Sammi says. "They can't

keep starving us like this."

Tyson gets up to open the small refrigerator where employees are allowed to keep their lunches. We looked in it earlier, so I know he knows it's pointless, but he does it anyway. "Still just the Diet Coke in here," he says. "Whose initials are these, anyway?"

I shake my head. "I need sugar."

"I totally agree. That diet crap is worthless," Gabe agrees.

"No . . . I . . . need sugar." I lean forward, pressing my hot cheek to the tabletop.

"Are you all right?" Zaina asks.

I try to shake my head again, but it doesn't work very well. It's so unbearably hot in the room that everything seems hard. A high-pitched whining starts in my ears.

"Chloe?" Someone's hand lands on my back.

"Chloe, are you okay?" The voice sounds distorted and slow.

I try to tell them I need some sugar right away, but the words won't come.

"Chloe?" The voice is closer now. Much closer. I open my eyes and find Tyson looking at me from just inches away. "What's wrong?"

"Diabetic," I whisper.

"You're diabetic?" he asks.

I nod as much as I can.

His eyes go wide. "Are you high or low?" he asks.

*Low.* My mouth forms the shape of the word, but I can't make any sound come out.

"We need to get her something to eat. Now." He stands, and I find myself staring at his pants. I close my eyes.

Their voices whirl around me, too fast to keep track, and then someone is lifting me by the shoulders. My head comes last, like it's stuck to the tabletop with glue.

"God, she's covered in sweat," a voice says.

"Chloe? Open your mouth."

My tongue makes a clicking sound when I open. I feel something against my lips and struggle to open my eyes. Tyson again.

"Hey!" He smiles encouragingly. "I'm going to put this on your tongue."

Suddenly, I feel something grainy fall into my mouth. Deep in my jaw, something twinges in reaction to the pure sweetness. It's a packet of sugar. When the tiny avalanche of crystals stops, I close my mouth, willing the glucose to go straight to my blood.

"Another?" Tyson asks, shaking one of the little packets.

I nod once and then his fingers are on my jaw, steadying me as he brings the paper envelope to my lips.

"Is this going to work?" Zaina asks.

"Yeah, but it'll take a few minutes."

"What should we do?" Micah asks. "Should I call nine-one-one?"

Adrenaline powers me to gasp out, "No!"

"She'll be okay," Tyson says. "Let's lie her down."

Zaina wrinkles her nose. "On the floor?"

"I don't see another option, do you?"

"We should at least spread out some coats or something."

My head is propped against somebody's body. Not sure who or what part of them I'm leaning against, but it's easier to let it rest there with my eyes closed while I wait for the hit of sugar to do its job. It's not going to be enough, but it's a start.

"Chloe." Tyson's voice again. My stomach flutters, but I don't think I'm going to puke this time. "Come on, let's lay you down." He hooks me under the armpits, and the world tilts crazily and then I'm lying on the floor, with a slim layer of parkas beneath me. There's something lumpy under my lower back, but I don't have the energy to rearrange it.

"Chloe? Are you okay?" Zaina's voice.

I struggle to open my eyes and fight for focus while two Zainas stretch out and snap back together.

"I'm okay." My voice is choked with the unfamiliar coating of sugar in my throat.

"What do you need?" Gabe's face pops into view, upside down. I roll my eyes up to see him.

"My monitor," I croak. "In my locker."

Can this really be happening? All the time I spent not talking about my diabetes, and now I'm in the middle of a hypoglycemic attack on the floor of the Break Room?

"What's your combination?" Sammi asks from across the room.

I think hard, my fingers moving with muscle memory as I bring the combination up from the depths of my brain. I tell her the three numbers and hear the telltale clunks of the lock releasing and the door opening. It takes a little back and forth, but she finds the meter in my bag and brings it to me.

"I can do it," Tyson says when I reach for it with violently shaking hands.

"No—" I start, but he cuts me off.

"My grandma has diabetes. I've done this a million times. This is one of the arm ones, right?"

I nod.

He's gentle as he pushes back my sleeve. A few seconds

later there's a slight pinch from the lancet and then the feathery pressure of the test strip against my skin. He's going to be a fantastic vet someday. I open my eyes again, finding everyone that I can see focused intently on the meter. The electronic beep announces a result.

"Forty-two," Gabe reads. "What does that mean?"

"It means she needs more food."

It means I was in dangerous territory before the sugar. Way too low. It's a miracle I didn't pass out completely.

"Well, let's get her some freaking food," Sammi says.

"The fridge is empty," Tyson reminds her.

"It's a grocery store; I'm sure we can find something," she retorts. I don't have to see her to know she's rolling her eyes.

"I'll go with you," Gabe says. "What do you want, Chloe? Cookies or something?"

"She needs protein, not sugar," Tyson says.

"Wait. What?" Sammi says.

"Protein?" Tyson says slowly.

"A turkey sandwich," I whisper. "Sugar-free yogurt . . . some cheese or . . ."

"Too complicated," Sammi declares. "We'll just bring you along."

"What?" I crane my neck, trying to see her. The sugar

is already starting to work and my eyes can focus a lot better. The ringing in my ears is quieting, too.

"She's shaking like crazy," Tyson says. "She can't move."

Sammi frowns. "Fine, we'll put her in a cart."

TOP TEN MOST ANNOYING THINGS PEOPLE SAY WHEN
THEY FIND OUT I HAVE DIABETES

10. "Wow, you don't look like you have diabetes!"

9. "I bet you miss sugar."

8. "I thought only old people got diabetes."

7. "Oh my God, I couldn't poke myself! I hate needles!"

6. "How do you get rid of it?"

5. "Is your foot going to fall off?"

4. "Aww, it must be because you're so sweet!"

3. "Does it bother you when people eat cake in front of you?"

2. "Is it the bad kind?"

1. "But diet soda's so bad for you!"

The cart is padded with coats, but it's still not exactly com-
fortable. The child seat is digging into my shoulders, and

there's no good way to arrange my legs. But the others are so pleased with themselves, I'm not about to complain.

It took some fancy talking on Sammi's part to convince Kris I didn't need an ambulance when she ran out to bring a cart back to the Break Room, but he cooperated. Not only that, he told us to take what we needed and not worry about the cost. The registers are closed, but as Sammi pointed out, nobody wants to be responsible for sending a minor to the hospital because they wouldn't give her any food in a *grocery store.*

Now we're headed back into the store, me in my squeaking cart, the others on foot.

The night crew has finished, and the work lights are out. It's still relatively bright up front, but as soon as we pass the floral department, the walls behind the bakery cast long, dark shadows over the floor.

"Whoa." Gabe hesitates.

"Afraid of the dark?" Sammi teases. "You can hold my hand if you need to." She extends one hand, wiggling her fingers. I expect him to knock it away, or make some sarcastic remark, but he doesn't.

"I'm skeered!" he jokes, grabbing her hand and crowding her like a toddler in a thunderstorm. Too bad he's a good eight inches taller than her.

"What a baby," she says.

He laughs, and slips back into an easy stroll. But he doesn't let go of her hand. Instead, he leads the way, giving her a tug to follow. "Never fear, young maiden, you'll be safe with me!"

"Gross," Sammi says, but she doesn't pull away.

"You said turkey, right, Chloe?" Gabe pauses at the gap between the wall and the deli cases.

"Yeah, but shouldn't we just grab a pack of Oscar Meyer or something?"

"We could, but . . . come on, we've got the run of the deli. Let's get something decent."

"Are you sure?"

He doesn't answer, but drags Sammi with him to the double swinging doors behind the display cases to the prep room. With no Christmas music coming from the PAs and no customers making a din, we can almost make out the sound of them moving around in the dark room. After a moment a light flicks on.

"Is there anything else we can do for you, Chloe?" Micah asks.

I hate being the center of attention like this, but I do have a request. "I'm really thirsty."

"Water!" he says excitedly. "I can do that. I'll be right back!"

Tyson comes around to the end of the cart and leans his forearms on the edges, looking down at me with an unreadable expression.

"What's wrong?" I ask.

"Why didn't you tell me you have diabetes?" Is that hurt in his voice?

"It never came up."

"If I'd known, I would have . . ." He shrugs.

*Would have what?* "It's okay."

Someone else approaches, standing on my right. It's Zaina with a wet paper towel in her hand. "You're sweating." She lifts the cloth hesitantly, so I nod and she sets to work blotting my face.

After a minute, Micah returns with a bottle of water from one of the Grab-and-Go coolers near the salad bar. Tyson helps me sit up to have a few sips. My parched mouth goes crazy at the sensation and I shiver. Tyson eases me back, but his hand stays behind my neck.

I should be blushing from all this ridiculous attention. But I can't seem to muster up the energy to feel anything but grateful for their help.

Tyson's thumb strokes the side of my neck and I shiver again.

"Are you cold?" Zaina asks.

"I'm fine."

"My sister has JRA," Micah says, out of nowhere.

"What?" Tyson takes the word right out of my mouth.

"JRA," he repeats. "Juvenile rheumatoid arthritis. It's this disease that makes all her joints get swollen up. Bunch of other stuff, too, so she's sick a lot. She has to take this special medicine that goes in an IV. We have a nurse come to the house once a week to give it to her."

"Why are you telling us this?" Zaina asks.

"I don't know. I just thought it might make Chloe feel better."

"I'm sorry your sister is sick," I say. "But it doesn't really make me feel better. I know other people have it worse than me."

"No, I—" Micah shakes his head. "I just meant that you're not alone, is all."

"Oh. Well, thanks, I guess."

We fall into an awkward silence, and I can't find a place to keep my eyes. Zaina stands to my right, Micah near my feet, and Tyson at my left shoulder. Even though it's dark, I can't bear the way they're all staring at me. But I don't have the strength to move yet. Plus, they're all trying so hard to be nice. I decide to close my eyes instead.

All the while, Tyson's thumb keeps smoothing along my neck, the pressure just past the point of being ticklish. I wish I could lean into it. I want him to be touching me out of something more than concern for the stupid girl who forgot to eat her dinner. He's probably mentally petting a scared dog in his future vet clinic. "What is taking those guys so long?" he mutters after a while.

"Should I check on them?" Micah asks. "Maybe they got stuck in the walk-in cooler."

Before anyone can answer, the doors swing open and we watch Gabe emerge from the gloom with something really big cradled in his arms.

"Chloe, you weren't kidding about the protein. Did you know there's an entire ham back here with your name on it?"

I realize immediately that I never picked up the spiral-cut ham my mom ordered for Christmas dinner. I'd planned to do it at the end of the day, but the deli crew must have put it away when I didn't show up.

"Why do you have a ham with your name on it?" Gabe asks, hauling his prize up to balance on the edge of the cart.

"It's my mom's," I say. "I forgot to get it earlier."

"See? I told you it was hers," Gabe calls back to Sammi, who's carrying a few smaller things in her hands.

"Did you at least get some turkey?" Tyson asks.

"Right here," Sammi says around a mouthful of something. "And this." She holds up a black plastic tray of taco dip. "I figured we needed this."

I shrug. "Yeah, I guess that might work."

"No," she says. "We *need* it. *I* need it."

"You *need* it?" Micah repeats.

She nods. "I love this stuff."

Gabe grins. "I think that might be the first time I've ever heard you say you like something."

"I like plenty of things." She says this with a scowl.

"Here, Chloe. Have a ham," he says, letting the big slab of meat tilt toward me in the cart.

"Hang on!" I get my hands under it just in time to catch the monster, but it still thumps onto my lap and rolls down my upraised knees to sock me in the gut. An "Oof!" rushes out of me.

"Way to go, genius," Sammi says. "We're supposed to be helping the girl."

"I'm okay," I croak.

Tyson lifts the ham away from me, stowing it on the bottom rack instead. "Better?"

"Thanks."

"Name five," Gabe says.

"What are you talking about?" Sammi asks, handing

me the stuff she brought from the deli prep room. There's a small zippered pouch of deli turkey, and like the good diabetic I am, I open it to down a mouthful.

Gabe continues, "You said you like plenty of things. Name five."

"Stop it. We've got to get Chloe more food." She goes behind me and the cart starts rolling.

Gabe doesn't let it go. "Can't do it, can you?"

"Taco dip," Sammi says above my head. "American Spirit cigarettes."

"Yuck," Gabe says cheerfully as we roll deeper into the store.

She ignores him and keeps ticking off items. "The Muppets, and . . ."

He pounces. "Ha! You can't do it!"

"Shut up! You didn't let me finish!"

"Because you can't think of anything."

"That is *not* true. I like plenty of things. I like dogs, and sleeping in, and the color green, and dragons, and snowboarding, and—"

"You snowboard?" he interrupts.

"A little." She stops at the head of aisle two. "We need tortilla chips."

"And cookies." He grins. "I only tried it once.

Snowboarding, I mean. I have never fallen on my ass so much in such a short amount of time."

I know he's not talking to me, but I can't help laughing. "No way. You?"

"Well, yeah. It's hard." He doesn't seem embarrassed at all. "But I think I'd be better at it if I tried again."

"I'd actually pay money to watch you fall on your ass," Sammi says. "Here we go." She stops the cart in front of a display of chips and stands on her toes, stretching for the right bag.

Gabe reaches up easily and brings it down to her level. "You'd be sorely disappointed."

"Somehow, I doubt that." She looks at the rest of us. "What else do you guys want?"

"I thought it was just for Chloe," Micah says.

"Don't you think we all deserve a little something after being held captive for"—she consults her watch—"two hours?"

I can hardly believe it's been that long. No wonder my sugar tanked.

Zaina sticks one finger in the air hesitantly. "I'd like a Coke."

"Now we're talkin'!" Sammi gets behind the cart again and pushes me toward the opposite end of the aisle.

"All right. I'll prove it to you." Gabe goes back to their conversation as if no one else had spoken. "We'll go snow-boarding together and I'll completely smoke your ass."

"Yeah, right."

"I'm serious. I'll school you so hard, you'll have a master's degree in shame."

"Shaming you, maybe." She turns up the next aisle, where cases of soda are stacked on the shelves beneath two-liters.

"Oh, that's it. We are definitely going."

"We'll see."

"We're going." He steps onto the end of the cart, staring at her over my head.

"I can't see, you big giant. Get off!"

"Say yes." He speaks softly.

Sammi stops the cart. "Yes."

"There. Was that so hard?"

"Yes," she repeats.

I feel like I'm peeping through a window at something private, but it's not like I can do anything about it. My cheeks are hot, though, and I really wish they'd remember I'm here.

Micah breaks the tension, asking, "Can we get Sour Patch Kids?"

Gabe grins and jumps off the end of the cart. "And Mountain Dew."

"And Oreos," Tyson says.

*"Allons-y!"* Sammi shouts, and suddenly the cart is moving at serious speed. I tumble to the side as we take a corner, and I have to brace myself with both hands.

"Sammi!" I squeak.

"Hold on!" Her feet thud against the floor for a few more steps and then the sound stops and she's riding the back of the cart, her head hanging forward so I can see the underside of her chin. And I'm laughing even though my hands are still shaking.

There's a *thump!* and Micah shouts, "Hey! Your ham!" which only makes me laugh harder. When the cart starts to slow, Sammi hops down and does a three-sixty. I shriek and close my eyes, and then we're on the move again, rushing through the dim aisles. The cart slows from time to time as Sammi jumps down to snatch something off a shelf or to get another running start.

We're careening through the store at a dizzying speed, with the others running after us. No one is faster than Sammi and her cart, though, and before I know it we're back in the snack-foods aisle.

"Ham! Dead ahead!" Sammi shouts, jumping off the

cart to swerve around the big roast still on the floor. The cart goes wild and slams into the bottom shelf, sending half a dozen or so family-size bags of chips to the floor. I get tossed from side to side in the process, but it's not so bad. I'm still laughing.

Until Mr. Solomon appears at the other end of the aisle, Kris just behind him.

"What are you doing?" he demands.

Sammi skids to a stop, making the cart shimmy before it runs out of energy. "Nothing," she says.

Solomon closes his eyes and rubs his temples. "Go back to the Break Room. I don't want to see you out here again."

"What a buzzkill," Sammi mumbles to me.

My eyes prickle. This is humiliating.

THINGS THAT ARE LESS AWKWARD THAN GETTING
CAUGHT RIDING THROUGH THE STORE IN A SHOPPING
CART IN FRONT OF YOUR (ANGRY) BOSSES

1. Newborn giraffes
2. Having your phone ring during a movie
3. Not remembering someone's name, so you have to wait for
   someone else to come up and hope they introduce themselves
   so you don't have to
4. Calling your teacher Mom
5. Being the only one in costume at a Halloween party
6. Sneezing on the casket at a funeral
7. Walruses on land
8. Walking in flippers
9. Opening a bathroom stall door when someone is already in it
10. Leaning in to hug someone who didn't mean to hug you

The cart squeaks rhythmically as we roll past Mr. Solomon. I try to stare straight ahead, but it's like I'm a magnet and he's a giant refrigerator. Just past his shoulder I meet Kris's eyes. He looks tired, and annoyed.

This is quite possibly the most awkward moment of my life.

"Miss Novak, I trust you are feeling better?" Solomon says, strolling after us.

I nod, my fingers curling reflexively around the little deli pouch of turkey in the bottom of the cart. The others shuffle by, doing a much better job of avoiding eye contact than I did. But there's still plenty of awkwardness ahead when Sammi steers the cart past the Self Checkout lanes, and then I have to get out while Solomon continues to stare at us.

When I stand on shaky legs in the unstable cart, it's clear I'm not going to be able to do this myself. I'm about to lower myself back down for another attempt when Gabe wraps an arm around my waist and scoops me out without even straining himself.

"Be careful!" Tyson cautions, taking me by both arms when I'm on my feet again. "You all right?"

I flush at the attention. "Fine."

Solomon looks at Micah. "Why are you carrying a ham?"

"It's Chloe's." He rotates it to show the sticker with my name on it. "See?"

Now Solomon looks back at me. "Is it really yours?"

"My mother ordered it." My voice wavers a bit. "For Christmas dinner."

"I see." His eyes shift to the various items in our cart and in the others' hands. "And did your mother order Mountain Dew as well?"

"No, sir."

"You do remember you're here because of stealing, correct?"

"I offered to buy them all a snack," Kris says out of the blue.

I steal a glance at Sammi, but she won't look back at me. She didn't say anything about Kris paying before.

"They're hungry, Gene." Kris steps forward, reaching back for his wallet. "It's been a long day. And Chloe was in pretty rough shape."

*I'm still not in great shape,* I want to say. My legs feel like cooked spaghetti under me and I'm glad Tyson is holding on to one of my arms.

Mr. Solomon has the grace to look a bit ashamed. "Of course."

"Here." Kris opens his wallet and extracts some money. "What do you think? Will forty cover it?"

"Twenty," Micah says. "The ham is prepaid."

For some reason that strikes the rest of us funny and I have to suck my lips between my teeth to keep from laughing. Sammi and Gabe aren't as successful, while Micah looks bewildered and Tyson smothers his laugh in a cough. Zaina manages to keep her eyes focused on the bosses with only the tilted corner of her mouth revealing her amusement.

Kris catches my eye and winks as he hands over the twenty. One of the knots in my stomach uncoils. He's not that mad.

Part of me expects Mr. Solomon to turn down the money. After all, he's the one holding a bunch of kids hostage in a grocery store. The least he can do is spare a few gummy bears and some soda. But he takes the twenty and pulls a money clip from his pocket. I watch him add the stiff bill to the outside of a fairly substantial stack of cash, and for the first time I wonder if he might have stolen the money himself.

Immediately, I dismiss the idea. Why bother accusing us when he could easily get away with it without even drawing any attention to the fact it was missing?

"I'd like you all to remain in the Break Room until the police get here."

"What if—" Sammi starts, but Gabe puts his arm around her shoulders and covers her mouth with his hand.

"Never mind," he says, shuffling toward the door so Sammi has no choice but to move along with him.

We scurry inside. Gabe doesn't release Sammi until the door is closed, and then she pulls away from him like an angry cat. "Don't you ever do that again!" she snaps.

"I was trying to spare us all a little unnecessary drama."

"I had a question!" she says.

He doesn't speak, but cocks his head and waits. After a moment she breaks eye contact.

"Fine. But don't ever do that again, or I will hurt you. Do you understand?"

"Yes. You're very big and scary." He rolls his eyes.

Her face goes dark for a flash, but she seems to think better of whatever she was planning to say or do. She rocks back and says, "Damn straight."

Tyson says, "Can we eat already?" and then everyone is moving toward one of the tables. We lay out everything we've got and the feasting begins.

I stick with my turkey at first, knowing I need it, even though there are so many other things I'd rather have. There's hardly any talking for a bit as we chow down. Watching the others dig into the M&M cookies from the Bakery section has me sorely tempted to take one for myself, but I know I can't. The two packets of sugar already in my system are going to put my insulin to the test as it is. They don't need to see me shoot up into ketoacidosis after nearly passing out from low blood sugar.

"We should have gotten some French onion dip and potato chips," Gabe says around a mouthful of something.

"Next time we get locked up in the grocery store, we'll start with that," Sammi says.

As the food starts working its magic on my body, I realize how foggy my brain has been for a while now. The shakes and sweating stop, the pounding in my head is gone, and I feel in command of myself once more. It's a good feeling.

"Thanks, you guys," I say when I'm starting to feel full.

"You're welcome," Micah says.

"Just do us a favor and don't ever let it get that bad again before you tell us you need to eat." Tyson smiles at me.

"Right." For once, I don't turn all red and blotchy. I think I may have managed to fill up my embarrassment tank for the day.

After a little more snacking, everyone is starting to slow down and I decide to refocus on the matter at hand.

"Micah, how much room would all that money have taken up?" I ask.

Just like Tyson and Gabe did earlier, he doesn't really answer. "That depends on the denominations and conditions of the bills. For example, if everyone put in hundred-dollar bills, there would only be a hundred of them, but—"

Sammi flaps a dismissive hand. "Yeah, we get it. Why are you asking, Chloe?"

"I was trying to imagine how someone could empty the entire box without anyone noticing. If it were a lot of small bills, like singles, it would be a lot, wouldn't it? A grocery bag full, I would think."

"You'd think you'd notice if someone was walking around with a big bag of cash," Tyson agrees.

"Not if they did it after the store was closed," Gabe says.

"*Or*—" I lean into the word, proud of my lightbulb moment. "What if they didn't take it all at once?"

Tyson sucks in a breath, like he's preparing a rebuttal, but nothing comes out. "That could have happened."

"Who had the key?" I wonder aloud.

"Solomon did, but other than that, who knows?"

"Management, probably," Zaina says.

"Maybe not, though," I say. "Why would anyone need to get inside the box before today? It didn't matter how much money was in there, does it? As long as there was still enough room for people to drop in their donations, right?"

"So, what are you saying?" Zaina asks.

"I—" I open my mouth, hoping for another breakthrough conclusion to slip out, but it turns out I don't have one. "I'm not sure."

"It had to be somebody who knew how to pick a lock, then," Tyson says. "Without breaking it."

"Who knows how to do that?" Gabe says.

"I do!" Micah volunteers.

Sammi is gaping at Micah. "You?"

"Sure. I learned how on the internet."

"Oh." Gabe slumps. "Anybody can watch a video, Micah."

"No, I can do it," Micah insists. "I practiced and everything. Padlocks are actually really easy."

"You're kidding."

"Not at all." His face lights up. "Did you know there are competitions for lock picking? It's called locksport."

Everyone looks at him blankly.

"Really," he insists. "It's a thing."

"Show us," Sammi says.

"I don't have a padlock." Micah looks around as if one might appear.

Sammi doesn't speak, but sticks one hand out, pointing to the employee lockers. Most of them are closed with combination locks, but there are a few padlocks in the bunch.

"Oh." Micah blanches. "Do any of you have one of them?"

We all shake our heads. It's easier to have a combination lock than to try to remember where your key is.

"I don't feel right breaking into someone else's locker without their permission," Micah says.

"Just unlock it," Sammi says. "You can close it up again. No one will even know."

Micah fidgets in his seat. "I don't know. . . ."

"I told you he couldn't do it," Gabe says.

"No, I can do it. I just don't know if I should."

"Come on, Micah. We won't tell."

This goes on for a while, with Sammi and Gabe working on Micah. The rest of us stay quiet. It's not that I think he shouldn't do it—I actually really want to see him do it—but I feel like I *should* be opposed to it, considering what we're already here for.

". . . need a hairpin," Micah says. "I don't have one of those."

"I do," Zaina volunteers.

Sammi spins around with a look of glee. "Excellent. Get it."

Zaina goes to her own locker and spins the combination into the lock. The interior of her locker is neat, with a small zippered case tucked in one corner. She searches it and brings out a black bobby pin. "Will this do?" she asks.

"That'll work." Micah takes it from her and scans the bank of lockers for his target. Eventually he settles on one near the floor, so he can sit comfortably in front of it.

The rest of us crowd around him, trying to get a look at what he's doing. It's hard to see what his hands are up to in such a small space, but I can tell that he's broken the pin in two pieces. He works one piece into the lock and bends it, then fishes it back out to use as a tool in concert with the other.

I hold my breath, waiting, and after a moment, I'm rewarded with a faint click.

Micah flicks his wrist and the lock opens. He slides it out of the loop on the door and holds it up triumphantly.

"Ho-ly crap," Gabe says. "You actually did it."

"I told you I could." Micah smiles. "It's easier with a thin piece of plastic—"

"Yeah, yeah." Sammi cuts him off, dropping to a

crouch beside him. "Now let's see whose locker this is."

"No! We're not opening it!" Micah slams his hand on the door. It bangs into place, making the rest of the locks chatter against the metal.

"Oh, come on. What's the big deal?" Sammi says. "Aren't you at least curious?"

"You promised we would put the lock back on," Micah protests.

"I didn't *promise*," Sammi reminds him.

"Sammi," Zaina says. "Don't upset Micah."

Sammi seems surprised to be chastised by the usually quiet Zaina. She rocks back on her heels and holds her hands up in surrender. "All right. Put the lock back on, Micah."

With a sigh of relief, he does.

"Would you show me how to do that?" Gabe asks.

"Are you planning on doing something illegal?" Micah asks.

Gabe appears to think about it. "Probably not."

"I won't teach you unless you promise not to use the knowledge for evil." Micah is serious, even though the rest of us crack up.

Gabe draws in a breath, holds it, squinting at Micah for a moment, then lets it all out in a rush. "I can't promise that."

"Then I'm not going to teach you." Micah crosses his arms.

"Fine," Gabe drawls. "I just thought it would be a cool thing to know. The kind of thing you can bust out at a party or something."

"Stupid human tricks?" I supply.

"Exactly."

"I've never picked a lock at a party," Micah assures him.

"Have you ever even been to a party?" Sammi asks.

"I was at my grandparents' anniversary party just last month, but that's not what you mean, is it?" he says.

Tyson laughs. "You did not just say that."

"What?" Micah asks.

"You're hilarious," Gabe says.

My cheeks get hot on his behalf. "Don't listen to them, Micah. I think you're very sweet."

"Thank you, Chloe."

"Lock picking isn't a stupid human trick anyway," Tyson says. "It's a skill. Stupid human tricks are more . . ."

"Stupid?" I supply.

"I've got one!" Sammi announces. "Watch this." She gets up and backs away from the rest of us until she has a wide circle of empty space. Then, without warning, she flips onto her hands. Her legs go up and coins fall out of her pockets, plinking to the ground in all directions.

"Woo-hoo!" Micah cheers, initiating a clap that gets us all going.

"Wait!" Sammi grunts. Once she has her balance, she starts walking on her hands. She makes it about four paces before she overbalances and flings herself back to her feet. She straightens, sticking her arms up. "Ta-da!"

"Not bad. Not bad!" Gabe nods while we all continue to clap.

"Again, that's more of a skill," Tyson says.

Sammi juts her chin at Tyson. "All right, then, Mr. Expert. What can you do?"

He hesitates.

"What is it?" I'm delighted at the idea he has a hidden talent.

"Out with it!" Sammi commands.

Without speaking, Tyson gets to his feet. He tilts his head from side to side, making his neck crack, and takes a few steps in place. Then he shakes out his arms.

"Do it already!" Gabe shouts.

Tyson grabs his right wrist in his left hand and swings his arm up and over his head. When he brings it down behind his head, his shoulder bulges unnaturally, then suddenly it's flat again and his arm is all the way behind his back.

Everyone gasps and cringes as he does a rolling motion with his torso and the arm pops back up to a normal position. He brings it around to the front and lets go of his wrist, spreading his arms wide in presentation.

"I think I'm gonna puke," Gabe declares, looking decidedly green in the face.

"Totally sick!" Sammi obviously isn't grossed out at all.

"Does that hurt?" I ask.

"It's like a really intense stretch," he says. "I can't do it over and over again, but it's not bad if I just do it once or twice."

"Oh my God."

"That was disgusting," Gabe says. The green pallor is fading, but he still looks shell-shocked.

"Come on. Who else has something?" Tyson asks.

"I do," I say. "It's not as good as that, but it's kind of cool."

"What?"

"Okay, you have to pay close attention." I take off my glasses, instantly turning everyone into flesh-colored blobs. "Watch my eyes." I blink a few times to get them good and lubricated, then with intense concentration, I make my left eye go to the corner while the right stays staring straight ahead.

One of the colored blobs jumps back. "What the hell was that?" It's Sammi. "Do it again."

"Okay. Hang on." I close my eyes and straighten up in my seat. Repeating this trick is always harder after the first time. I don't know why. If I do it a bunch of times, I end up with a massive headache, but it's worth a time or two for the gross-out factor.

Opening my eyes, I repeat it and Sammi jumps again.

"That is just unnatural," she pronounces.

"Creepy," Zaina agrees.

I put my glasses back on. "All right, then, what can you do?" I ask Zaina.

"Besides speak three languages?" she teases.

"Yeah, besides that," Micah says without a trace of sarcasm.

"I can do this." She stands, her back very straight, and slowly raises one foot to touch her opposite knee, like a ballet dancer. Then it comes up higher, until she can grab it with her hand, and continues to rise until she's holding her foot above her head. Her knee and elbow are fully extended, and while she bobbles a bit to keep her balance on her other leg, the feat is very impressive. We all applaud.

"All right, that just leaves you, Gabriel," Sammi says.

Gabe sighs. "There's one thing I can do."

"I demand a demonstration." She thumps the table.

"De-mon-stra-tion," Tyson chants, pumping his fist.

I pick up the chant, then Micah and Zaina do, too.

"Yes!" Sammi cheers. "Show us. Show us or we'll all doubt your manhood for the rest of your life."

He gives her an "oh please" look.

She quirks her eyebrows at him and pokes him in the ribs. "Show us!"

"Fine." He brings his hands up to his face and flips his upper eyelids so we can see the insides.

"Ew!" I say without a thought.

Sammi cheers loudly, sticking both arms up in victory.

Gabe scrubs his face, righting his lids and looking embarrassed. "I told you I couldn't do anything cool."

The door to the store opens and Kris pokes his head in. "What are you guys doing in here?"

"Nothing." Sammi lets her arms drop.

"We're just talking," I say.

"Solomon called the police again. They said they'll be here in ten minutes." His mouth opens again like he wants to say something more, but he just nods and lets the door drop shut.

"Finally!" Zaina says.

"I can't believe I ate all that crap when I've got my

grandma's cooking waiting for me at home." Tyson sighs.

"Just eat more," Gabe says with a shrug.

Tyson makes a tsking sound. "I'm gonna have to. My grandma doesn't let people come to dinner without eating."

I let their words drift over me, but this time it's not about my blood sugar. This time, I'm thinking about the missing money. Ten minutes to figure this out.

I pull out my notebook again and jot down some thoughts.

- Potentially $10,000
- Mostly small bills
- Could have filled a grocery bag
- No damage to the lock—picked?
- Who has a key?
- Was the money taken all at once or every day?
- Someone accused us of stealing it, either one or all of us working together
- Everyone claims innocence
- Why did Solomon let all the other employees go? Why isn't everyone being fingerprinted?

I look up at the others. "Who do you think said we did it?"

"Who knows?" Gabe sighs.

"When in doubt, blame Agnes," Sammi says.

"But why would he believe Agnes?" I wonder.

"Because she's worked here since dinosaurs roamed the Earth?" Gabe suggests. "Because she's actually the soul of the store itself that only manifests in human form during regular business hours?"

Sammi laughs, a staccato burst of her *heh*s all stuck together.

Agnes doesn't seem like the culprit to me — not the thief or the one who accused us. I tap my pen on the end of the notebook and rack my brain for any details I might have missed.

"Has anyone noticed someone with something new lately? Something expensive?"

Everyone shakes their heads.

"The only person around here who has anything even remotely cool is Kris," Gabe says. "His car kicks ass."

Although I don't share his love of Kris's old red sports car, I can at least agree with his assessment of the rest of the employees. The people who work here aren't exactly rolling in spending money. A lot of them are actually retired people who either can't or don't want to stop working. They're not the type to come in with fancy watches or expensive cars.

Maybe I'm being judgmental. Maybe they've got giant flat-screen TVs, or designer wardrobes when they're not in their GoodFoods uniforms. Heck, they could have robot butlers for all I know.

"Did you know Kris is the owner's son?" Zaina volunteers.

"What?" I had no idea. I'm not the only one, judging from the look on the others' faces.

"How do you know?" Tyson asks.

"He told me." She looks down at her lap. "That's why he's a manager even though he's so young."

"How old is he?" Gabe asks.

"Twenty-one," she says.

"I had no idea," Sammi says.

"Neither did I," Micah says.

"Is it supposed to be a secret or something? Why did he tell you?" Tyson asks.

Zaina shakes her head, and for a moment, I think she's going to pull back inside herself and we'll never know. But then she sighs softly and straightens up to face us. "Because he wanted to impress me."

"What do you mean?" Micah asks.

"He's . . . interested in me."

My first thought is *Duh,* because she's the most beautiful human on the planet.

"Why do you say that?" Tyson asks.

"He told me." Her nose wrinkles.

"What did he say?" Sammi asks.

Zaina swallows hard. "He says a lot of things. Once he told me he can't wait for my eighteenth birthday so it's legal for him to want me."

My lips curl into a sneer. "Eww. Seriously?"

"*Kris?*" Sammi says. "Our Kris?"

Zaina nods. "He's always standing too close to me, or touching me." At this, her eyes glaze with tears.

"He probably thinks he's being funny," Gabe says.

"Why don't you tell him to back the hell off?" Sammi asks.

"I can't." Two fat tears slide down her cheeks.

"Why not?" Sammi demands. "I'd shove my elbow into his gut." She mimics the action.

Zaina's eyes close and her beautiful face creases. She sniffles quietly and wipes at her eyes. Finally, she whispers, "Because he caught me stealing."

REVELATIONS THAT HAVE SHOCKED ME LESS THAN
ZAINA ADMITTING TO STEALING
1. There is no Santa.
2. There is no evidence that Humpty Dumpty was an egg.
3. The Easter Island heads have bodies underground.
4. There are more bacteria cells in your body than actual body cells.
5. My dad was married once before meeting my mom.

The front legs of Gabe's chair thunk back to the ground as he leans forward. "*You* stole the money?"

"No!" Zaina's voice is choked with tears. "I told you I didn't have anything to do with that."

"Then what are you talking about?"

"This is so embarrassing." Zaina sighs. "My sister,

Layla, is . . . not a traditional Lebanese girl." Her accent gets much thicker and she makes a face that tells me she's imitating someone when she says "traditional Lebanese girl." "She wants to be completely American. My dad doesn't like it, but as my mother says, he's the one who brought us here."

Beside her Tyson reaches out to pat her shoulder, then pulls his hand back quickly. I have the same instinct to comfort her in some way, but with Tyson between us, it would be awkward to reach out. I have to settle for clenching my hands in my lap.

"My dad wants us to marry boys from other Lebanese families, but Layla likes to date American boys. And she—" Zaina stops and looks up at the boys for a moment, her chin tipping down at the same time. "She asked me to get her a pregnancy test while I was at work."

Micah gasps, and I find myself suppressing a laugh. It's his reaction, not Zaina's confession, that gets me. But I don't want her to think I'm laughing at her, so I snatch the bag of turkey off the table and shovel another pinch into my mouth even though I'm not hungry.

"It took me all day just to work up the courage to go into that section of the store." Her voice is so thick with tears, it's hard to hear her. "I put it in my apron pocket and went back to work. I thought I could just wait until the end of my shift and then I'd scan it and pay for it. But I couldn't make myself do it. It was too embarrassing." She brings one slim hand up to her mouth. It's shaking. "So I took it. I put it in my coat pocket and I tried to walk out of the store with it at the end of my shift."

"What happened?" I ask.

"Kris saw me do it." Fresh tears run along the tracks already on her cheeks.

"Did you get in trouble?" Micah asks.

She shakes her head. "No. He asked me to empty my pockets, so I did, but when he saw what I had, he just . . . smiled at me. He told me he'd let it go, and I was so humiliated I took it and left.

"Ever since then, he looks at me differently." She wraps her arms around herself, eyes closed. "I know what he must think of me. The things he says . . ."

"I'm so sorry," I say.

"I shouldn't have done it," Zaina whispers.

"Z," Tyson says softly. "It's okay." He covers her hand, still clenched on her shoulder, with his own. It's only for a moment, but my chest feels tight, watching him.

"Hey." Sammi pulls our attention to her side of the table. She has her arms crossed and one ankle hooked on the opposite knee. The picture of disinterest, but her blue eyes are focused directly on Zaina.

Zaina looks over slowly, cautiously.

"Screw that," Sammi says.

"What?"

"Screw feeling bad about it. You did what you had to do. It's not your fault Kris is a big perv." She rolls her eyes. "Men are pigs."

"Hey!" Gabe protests, but it's weak.

"I should have paid for it," Zaina says. "I had the money, but it was too humiliating."

"Forget about it, okay?" Sammi says. "Put five bucks in your drawer next time you work. Then you don't owe that bastard a thing. You can kick him in the nuts with a clear conscience."

"Oh, it was more than five," Zaina says in all seriousness. "I took one of the digital ones. Did you know they cost twenty dollars?"

Sammi tosses back her head, laughing. A real, full-on belly laugh, complete with shaking shoulders. It's infectious, and soon we're all cracking up.

Everyone except Zaina. She's smiling, though. It's impossible not to. "I don't see what's so funny," she says.

"Oh, man." Sammi wipes her eyes. "I don't know why,

but it makes me so happy that you went for the expensive kind."

Zaina blushes. "I wanted to make sure it worked."

That makes Sammi laugh even harder. "So, was she?"

Zaina looks confused.

"Your sister. Was she pregnant?"

"No." Relief floods her face. "I don't know what she would have done. What my father would have done."

"Why haven't you said anything before?" I ask. "About Kris, I mean."

"You all seem to like him so much." She lifts one shoulder in a half shrug. "I didn't know what to say."

To be honest, I'm not sure how I would have reacted before today. It's still hard to imagine Kris being all sleazy like that, but if I really think about it, I have seen him standing very close to her. Practically breathing down her shirt. I always assumed she liked the attention.

I feel awful. There's not much I can say to make it better, but I might as well give her a show of solidarity. I blurt out my own confession. "I crashed a bunch of carts into a car today."

"You did what?" Tyson demands.

I expect Sammi to hush me, but she just says, "You definitely did."

I tell them the story. How I'd wanted to help, and ended up putting us all at risk. And how I'd been all cagey in Solomon's office because I felt so guilty about it.

"No wonder he's so suspicious of us," Gabe says.

"I'm sure that's not the only reason," Tyson says. I expect him to give me a soothing pat on the hand like he did for Zaina, but none comes.

"So that makes three criminals among us," Sammi declares. "A thief"—she points to Zaina—"a vandal"—she points to me—"and a terrible cashier." Her finger moves to Micah, which makes everyone laugh.

"Might as well add me to the list," Gabe says. "I kind of assaulted the bell ringer today."

Sammi turns to him with interest. "You what?"

"It wasn't my fault," he says. "I was in Produce, which I hate, when Kris told me to go get carts. And I hate, hate, hate getting carts. I mean, I took the test to be a cashier mainly so I could avoid getting carts."

"Is there anything you don't hate about working?" Tyson asks.

Gabe ignores him and continues. "But I had to go because Sammi got hurt. So, actually, this is all your fault, *Samantha*."

"Bite me, *Gabriel*."

"Anyway, I get outside, and the guy is all *ka-ching, ka-ching, ka-ching, ka-ching.*" He makes little circles with his head like the sound is making him dizzy. "I don't know about you guys, but I'm about ready to kill myself every time I hear that sound after the last two months. And it's all nasty outside and nobody's even stopping long enough to look at the idiot with the bell, much less put anything in his bucket. But there he is, wedged into the corner next to a garbage can. He's not even close to the red bucket, but he's still clanging away with the damn bell."

He moves his hand like he's holding the bell. "*Ka-ching, ka-ching, ka-ching, ka-ching.* So I'm like, 'Really, dude? Why don't you just pack it in?' He tells me his shift isn't over, and I go, 'Nobody's gonna stop in weather like this.' And he's all, 'I have a job to do.'"

It's amusing to watch Gabe tell the story since he turns his head back and forth to play each part.

"So I get a bunch of carts, and it's frigging disgusting out there, and everyone's rushing so the carts are all a big tangled mess because nobody's pushing them in all the way, and I can't even use the Mule because it's so slushy out there. . . ." He fades off into an annoyed huff.

"Anyway, the whole time this guy is just going to town with the damn bell. *Ka-ching, ka-ching, ka-ching, ka-ching.* It's like I have a drill in my brain. I'm giving him dirty looks every time I go past, and this one time, he gives the bell a little extra *ting-a-ling*, so I know he's being a dick to me on purpose. Then he starts doing it every time.

"Four times, I pass this guy and he's shaking his bell right at me like an asshole. And I *hate* doing carts, and I hate it even worse when it's raining outside. The guy had to be stopped."

Everyone is leaning forward, waiting to hear what happens next.

"So on my last trip in, I grab his bell and chuck it into the parking lot. And he's all, 'What the hell is your problem?' and I'm like, '*You* are my problem!' And he goes, 'I ought to report you!' but he's out in the slush looking for his bell, so I'm just like, 'It was an accident!' all nice like that, and I push the carts in and then I'm gone." He makes a speeding-off gesture with one hand.

Sammi is doubled over with laughter by this time. "Oh. My. God. That is my favorite story of all time."

"I was pissed," Gabe says defensively.

"I wish I could see that on video!" she howls.

"That might be Top Ten All-Time material," Tyson agrees.

"You think?" I ask. "That would be a record, if we had

two All-Time additions in one day."

"Three," Gabe says. "Unless you're somehow not counting the fact that we've been locked up in work detention for hours."

"Okay, yeah, that's pretty weird, too," I agree.

"Not to mention being accused of stealing," Tyson adds.

"It's been a weird day."

"I cannot believe we are still sitting here," Sammi says.

"My parents must be going crazy," Micah says. "I know they're waiting to start Christmas Eve stuff until I get home."

"Mine, too," I say. "I can't wait to see my brother, too."

"Mine probably started without me," Sammi says.

"My parents are going to a cocktail party at the neighbor's house tonight," Gabe says. "They're probably happy I'm not home so they don't have to feel guilty about leaving me behind."

"Don't you have any brothers or sisters?" I ask.

"One of each. Both older. A lot older," Gabe says. "My sister is spending Christmas with her husband's family in Colorado this year, and my brother would rather be out with his friends anyway."

"So you're going to be alone tonight?" Micah asks.

"Probably."

"You can come to my house if you'd like," Micah offers. "My parents always invite over people with nowhere to go on Christmas."

Gabe studies him for a second. "You know, I just bet they do."

"So, do you want to come?" Micah asks.

"No. But thanks. It's a nice offer." Gabe shrugs, and brings his foot up to his seat so he can worry at the hole in his sneakers with one fingertip.

No one says anything for a while, and I'm starting to feel uncomfortable.

"I still don't think we should have to be fingerprinted," Sammi says.

"I don't really care at this point if it means we can get out of here," Gabe says.

"I think my fingerprints are already on file," Micah says. "My parents had it done at a safety fair when I was younger."

"Do you think they'll still look the same?" I wonder, turning over my hands to look at the whorls on my own fingertips.

"Mine are on file, too," Sammi says suddenly.

I admit it. My thoughts go straight to all kinds of

delinquency. I imagine Sammi with a can of spray paint in her hand, or behind the wheel of a car at age twelve. She fits easily into any of those pictures in my head.

"All foster kids get printed," she says. "It's part of the deal."

"You're a foster kid?" I ask.

"No." She looks down her nose at me. "I got adopted when I was eight."

I don't know what to say to that, so I pull my lower lip between my teeth. Like I want to show her that my mouth is too busy to speak.

"That's cool," Tyson says. "I've heard it's tough for older kids to get adopted."

"I've lived with my parents since I was six," she explains.

"Do you like them?" Micah asks.

Sammi shrugs. "They're all right. They're parents."

The desire to ask about her real parents burns on my tongue, but for once I'm able to keep quiet.

"So, you're kind of a cliché, aren't you?" Gabe asks.

"Excuse me?"

"You know, the foster kid with the chip on her shoulder." He grins. "I like it."

"Shut up, Mr. Golden-Boy-Who-Can't-Stand-Up-to-His-Father."

Gabe throws back his head, laughing. "Well played."

"So, what, that doesn't bother you?" she says.

"Nah." He lifts an imaginary cup in one hand. "A toast to being royally screwed up. Thanks, Dad, I owe you one."

"You're sick," Sammi says.

"You like it," he replies. "Now come on, don't leave me hanging." He gestures with his invisible cup.

Sammi eyes him, but slowly raises a pretend cup of her own and bumps her curved fingers against his. "Clink," she says.

"Anyone else?" Gabe asks, looking around the table at us.

"I'm not screwed up," Micah says.

"Oh, yes, you are," Gabe says. "You don't even know how to have a normal conversation with other human beings."

"I don't?" Micah looks horrified.

"Definitely not." Sammi leans across the table with her imaginary cup still held aloft. "But on you, it works."

Micah's expression is decidedly kicked-puppylike, but he lifts his hand, mimicking her position. "All right."

"You too," she says to Zaina.

"Why me?"

"Anyone who is too embarrassed to buy a pregnancy

test on her own register is definitely screwed up," Sammi says.

Zaina flushes, but raises her hand.

"Both of you." Gabe looks at me and Tyson. "Hands."

"What did we do?" I ask.

"You"—he points at me with his noncup hand—"had a mental breakdown over putting a ding in someone's car because you can't figure out how to flirt like a normal human being. And you"—he points at Tyson—"you're so normal, you're obviously sick in the head."

My heart pounds in my ears. He didn't say Tyson's name, but you'd have to be an idiot not to know what he's talking about. My head is going to burst into flames. But I all I manage to whisper is, "Shut up, Gabe."

"Oh, please," Sammi says, insisting with her fake cup, "get in this thing already."

"What the hell," Tyson mutters, and lifts his own hand.

"Woo-hoo!" Gabe hollers.

"Come on, Chloe." It's Zaina who prods me, to my surprise. "Don't be the only one."

I can't move. It doesn't matter what the others are doing. It doesn't even matter what I might want to do. My body has a plan of its own, and that plan is to play possum.

Tyson turns, facing me, though his hand is still lifted to the center with the others'. "You too," he says.

I slowly raise my eyes to his, feeling like my nerves might rattle themselves clear of my skin any second.

*He knows. He knows, he knows, he knows.* This is so embarrassing.

But he smiles softly, and reaches for my arm with his free hand. When he catches my wrist, my paralysis is finally broken, and I let him bring my hand up to the group.

Gabe cheers again, echoed this time by Sammi and then Micah and even Zaina.

"Clink," Tyson says. A chorus of clinks moves through the group and then I let my body sag back into my chair. I still can't bear to look at Tyson. Yet every nanosecond, his presence seems to grow bigger. He is somehow getting larger and larger, and putting off more heat the longer I sit with my pulse pounding in my ears.

I don't know if it's been a few seconds or an hour of this agony when the main door opens and Kris comes in, followed by Mr. Solomon, and two police officers in uniform, their radios squawking.

I've never been so happy to see authority figures in my life.

## TRUTHS ABOUT PEOPLE AND COPS

1. Even downright nasty people can suddenly become slavering dogs when there is an officer of the law present.
2. You can suddenly remember every detail of driver's ed when you see a squad car in your rearview mirror.
3. Most people speak at least one octave higher than usual when talking to a cop.
4. Every single thing you've ever done wrong comes screaming back to you the minute a cop makes eye contact with you.

The officers, Reyes and Harper, put me on edge, even though I know I didn't steal the money. My mind insists on replaying the accident in the parking lot, convinced that they'll somehow know about it.

*Incidentally, we got a call from one of your customers earlier today.*

*Someone completely destroyed her car in your parking lot. As long as we were already coming, we figured we'd arrest the guilty party. And it just so happens we know it was you, Chloe Novak! You have the right to remain silent. . . .*

Mr. Solomon thanks the officers for coming out on Christmas Eve and goes on about how hard it must be to be on duty on the holiday. Sammi snorts softly at that one, and for once I have to agree with her assessment. Awfully nice of him to be so concerned about the cops when he's been holding six teenagers hostage.

Officer Reyes, a smallish woman with little enamel earrings shaped like Christmas presents, seems to be in charge of the pair. She does most of the talking anyway, while Harper, a big, young guy whose shoes are weirdly shiny for the middle of winter, scribbles things in a note-book.

They want to hear the details of what happened, and they are particularly interested in the fact that Mr. Solomon can't be exactly sure how much money was stolen. Reyes seems downright annoyed by that, actually.

Thinking about it again, the facts do seem more than a little vague.

Fact: The charity box had been sitting on the Customer Service desk, locked, since the day after Halloween.

Fact: The other boxes at the other GoodFoods stores had a lot more money than our box did.

Fact: Zaina could testify to putting in a twenty-dollar bill each time she worked, but there was no proof other than the video of her putting money in today.

Fact: Inside the box today, there was only one twenty-dollar bill.

Fact: The security tapes of the store, which delete automatically after forty-eight hours, showed at least twenty people at the Customer Service desk making movements that suggested they'd put money in, including Zaina.

Fact: The lock was undamaged and only Mr. Solomon had the key.

That's literally all we know. Everything else is guesswork.

"So, let me get this straight," Reyes says. "You *think* people put money into the box, but you can't be sure due to the angle of the camera."

"But I did," Zaina says. "Every time."

"And you say it was always a twenty-dollar bill."

"Yes."

"And you put these twenties in how many times?"

"I'm not sure," she says. "I think it was about twenty?"

"I estimated four hundred dollars," Micah pipes up.

Reyes ignores him. "And there was only one twenty-dollar bill in there when you unlocked it today."

Mr. Solomon nods. "I can show you the money."

"Sure. Let's take a look," she says. She follows Solomon into the manager's office.

I'm starting to doubt we'll be getting out of here quickly after all.

The radio on Harper's shoulder crackles with static, and we catch a few garbled words before he turns the volume down.

"Can you really make us get fingerprinted?" Sammi asks him.

He shifts his feet. "Not unless we arrest you."

"Are you going to arrest us?" she asks.

"Only if you did something illegal."

She nods. "Just checking."

"What do you care?" Gabe whispers to her. "I thought they already have your prints."

"You gotta know your rights," she says solemnly. "Fight the man."

Harper chuckles.

Kris clears his throat. "What if someone's fingerprints *are* found on the box?" he asks. "I mean, couldn't they have touched it sometime in the last two months?"

"And aren't there, like, a million fingerprints all over

money?" Sammi adds.

"Not exactly a million," Harper says.

"Still."

"We'll see what happens," he says.

The office door opens again and Reyes leads the way out. Solomon is behind her, carrying the oversized donation box.

"Miss Malak?" Reyes looks at Zaina. "Can you describe the money you put in the box?"

"What?" Tyson says softly, barely loud enough for me to hear. "It's a twenty-dollar bill."

Zaina swallows. "It was new," she says. "My mother always gets them from the bank so she can put a stamp of the *hamsa* on it as a blessing." She lays her hand on the table, palm up with her thumb curving out stiffly. It's a weird gesture—very unnatural.

"Could you identify it?" Reyes gestures for Solomon to open the box. When he grabs the lock to fit the key in, my heart leaps. Now there's no way my fingerprints will be the only ones on the casing! I want to do a victory dance.

He slips the padlock out of the clasp and lets it fall open, showing us the small collection of bills once more.

Zaina reaches out and uses one fingertip to knock a few other bills away from the crisp twenty. She coaxes it closer and, touching it as little as possible, flips it over to reveal a blue stamp in one of the emptier fields. It's a stylized hand with the middle three fingers straight together, and the thumb and pinkie curling out to the sides. It's beautiful, ornately decorated with flowers and scrolling lines.

"This is mine," she says. "All of them had this stamp on them."

"It's illegal to mark US currency," Micah says.

"Hush." Sammi gives him the stink eye.

"This is yours?" Reyes repeats.

Zaina nods. "Yes. Each one of the bills I put in had this mark on it."

"Does your mom do that with all her money?" I ask, leaning forward to look at the bill.

"Only for special reasons. Why?"

"I feel like I've seen this before. . . ." I squint, then close my eyes completely, willing my memory to suddenly become a perfect computer catalog of every bill I've ever seen. It's not easy, considering how much cash has passed through my hands since I started working the register. Not to mention I'm not a human computer.

I rub my fingertips together, trying to imagine a marked bill between them. We check new twenties for signs of authenticity. I would have paid attention to a crisp one like Zaina's describing.

The image tickles at the edge of my mind, but I can't

grab it. I open my eyes, frustrated.

Kris stands. "Can I use the bathroom?" he asks.

"You're not under arrest," Reyes says with a smirk.

"Well, then . . . excuse me. Nature calls." He gives an embarrassed smile, and heads for the door.

Everyone is fixated on the small blue stamp before us, like it holds the secrets to the universe.

Reyes sighs. "All right. Thank you. I guess we can go ahead and get a set of fingerprints from each of you, with your permission."

"Do we get to go home after you do that?" Gabe asks.

She nods. "Eventually."

"Whatever. Great. Take my prints. I don't even care." He holds his hands out in offering.

"Mine, too." I sigh, wishing I could have solved this before they arrived.

"You can take mine, too," Tyson agrees.

"Mine are already on this bill," Zaina says. "Are you going to arrest me?"

"We'll compare them to any we find on the interior of the box and the padlock. We can't arrest you for handling your own money."

"Then you can take mine, too."

Sammi sighs. "You already have mine."

"You can take mine again. I was just a kid last time I had them done," Micah says. "I didn't touch the box, though."

"Harper, why don't you start on that end—" Reyes points to me. "Mr. Solomon, we'll need to get a set from you, too, for elimination."

"Absolutely. Anything you need."

"I have to warn you, we can't make any promises," she says. "There might not be any useable prints on any of this stuff."

"What if that happens?"

Reyes props her hands on her belt. "Unfortunately, a lot of crimes like this go unsolved."

Officer Harper approaches me with a small white card in his hand. "I'm going to have you press your fingers on this—"

"Oh my God, Kris had one of your bills!" I shout, jumping to my feet. I nearly head butt the officer in the process, but I can't stop to worry about that.

"What?" The response comes from several people at once.

"Kris! Earlier! I saw him!" My hands jitter wildly in the air without my permission. "He had one of the things! Those! I saw it!"

"What are you saying?" Mr. Solomon asks.

I stumble over a few nonsensical syllables before spitting out, "Kris did it!"

They're staring at me in disbelief.

"I'm telling you!" I insist. "He had one of Zaina's twenties. In his wallet! When he paid for the food we took!"

"Who is Kris again?" Reyes asks.

"The guy who just walked out of here." Tyson points.

We turn as one, like a cartoon, looking at the exit.

"Harper," Reyes says, and without a word, Officer Harper jogs out. Reyes follows and we all watch the door swing shut behind her.

"Are you sure about this?" Gabe asks.

"Completely sure!" I shout. My volume control seems to be on the fritz. I've never been so excited in my life.

"There must be some explanation. . . ." Mr. Solomon is talking to himself, I guess, because he's already walking out the door.

We look at one another for a second, then all scramble after him.

Out in the store, Officer Reyes is near the main entrance, talking into her radio, and Solomon stands nearby with his hand pressed to his forehead.

"Where did he go?" I whisper.

"Where's Harper?" Tyson wonders.

"Bathroom?" Micah asks.

Gabe jogs off in that direction, and listens at the door to the men's room for a second before opening it. Even from a distance I can see the motion sensor light go on. No one else could be inside if the lights were off. Gabe shakes his head at us.

"I bet he went out the back," Tyson reasons. "That's where most of the employees park."

"That's probably where Officer Harper went, too," Zaina says.

"Come on." Gabe takes off again, this time running toward the frozen foods. The cases have gone dark again, but they flare to life as he passes them.

"Gabe!" Sammi hisses, running after him. "Don't!"

"That idiot's going to get himself hurt," Tyson says, but he takes off in the same direction.

I look at Zaina and Micah. "Well?"

"Let's go." Micah weaves through two checkouts and breaks into an all-out sprint toward the lighted path left behind by the others.

"This is not very smart," Zaina says as we both scurry after them.

"Nope," I agree.

"Why are we doing this?"

I try to shrug, but it's not very successful when you're running. "I don't know."

"All right."

We're both a little out of breath by the time we get to the back of the store—surprise, surprise. The entrance to the warehouse area is between cottage cheese and pork, and the double silver doors are still swinging. Not hard to tell where the others went.

I push one door open, getting a face full of cold, damp air. Zaina crowds close behind me, peeping around my shoulder.

"Where are they?" she says in a barely audible voice.

"I don't know." I listen, but the drone of the cooling units makes it hard to zero in on anything.

"Maybe by the loading dock," Zaina whispers.

We creep into the big, dimly lit room, close together for security. The dark shapes of dairy carts, shipping crates, and pallets make shadows and blind spots everywhere. Walking toward them feels dangerous and stupid.

"Do you really think Kris stole the money?" she asks.

"I'm pretty sure."

"But you could be wrong," she says.

"Then where is he?" I ask.

"Good point."

As we round a row of carts loaded with milk, I spot Sammi's blond hair lit against the general dimness of the room. She's hunkered down behind a large produce crate filled with flattened boxes. I put a hand out to still Zaina and we both drop into a crouch.

I try to duckwalk forward, but in the end I have to put my fingers on the ground and creep like some kind of woodland creature just learning to walk. I'm definitely not ready for a life as a ninja. Sammi turns when she hears our footsteps and holds a finger to her lips.

Zaina and I close the distance to her. She beckons me closer still and whispers in my ear, so soft I have to strain to hear.

"Kris is in here," she says.

I put my mouth to her ear. "Where is everyone else?"

"The cop is by the back door. The boys are—" She points in both directions away from us.

I relay the information to Zaina, her dark hair tickling my nose as I breathe the words into her ear. She goes wide-eyed.

"What are we going to do?" she asks.

Sammi shakes her head.

A movement to my right catches my eye and I get a

glimpse of Tyson sliding between two pallets.

"Where exactly is Kris?" I ask.

Sammi points at the crate we're crouched behind. *Two over*, she mouths. *I think*.

I feel strangely calm, even though my heart is racing. It's like my vision becomes clearer, my hearing sharper.

To our left, something metallic clangs and I hear a soft curse. If I had to guess, I would say it was Gabe, but I can't be sure. Then, straight through the crate, I hear shuffling sounds. Zaina grips my arm tightly.

"Kris?" Officer Harper calls out. His voice is nearly absorbed by the refrigeration units. They remind me of the deafening white noise on an airplane. "If you're in here, please come forward. I don't want you to get hurt."

More metallic sounds from the left. I lean back, squinting into the dark for any sign of what's causing it. The only light comes from caged fluorescents near the ceiling. They barely penetrate down by the floor.

The shuffling on the other side of the crate comes again, but this time it sounds farther away.

"Don't make this hard on yourself, Kris," Officer Harper calls.

"We shouldn't be here," Zaina breathes in my ear.

She's totally right, of course. We should have stayed in

the Break Room. But we're here now, and it seems like we might as well help. Or try to, anyway.

I look at Sammi and mime pushing the shipping crate. She smiles, nods, and applies her hands to it. I do the same and we give it a little force. It doesn't move much, but it does scuff an inch or so across the concrete floor. The shuffling sound comes back, louder this time and moving away.

"Again," Sammi whispers. We give it another push.

"Kris, I can hear you. You might as well cooperate. This will go a lot easier." Harper's radio crackles, and he speaks into it. It's too hard to hear what he's saying.

I get back to a crouch and run, hunched, in the direction I last saw Tyson. Zaina gasps when I move, but I don't stop until I reach the pallet where he disappeared. Then I squeeze through the same spot and nearly trip over him on the other side.

He grabs me by the arms and yanks me down. I fall into his lap with a grunt and he holds a finger to his lips. He pushes back stray hairs that have sprung loose from my ponytail, finding my ear to whisper, "What are you doing?"

I turn my head to speak into his ear, putting our cheeks together like we're slow dancing, except it's kind of

271

nerdy because the temples of our glasses click together. But nerds slow dance, too, right? "We shoved a crate a little bit before, and it got Kris to move. I think we can push him toward the cop."

"No way."

"Why not?"

His breath is hot against my cheek in contrast to the temperature of the cooler. "We should stay out of it."

"We're already in it." I ease back to look at him. We've never been this close before.

He licks his lips, and pulls me close to whisper once more. "I don't want you to get hurt."

My stomach turns somersaults of a new variety. "I don't want you to get hurt, either. But I want to get out of here, don't you?"

"All right." His lips brush against my ear, and I try not to shiver. "What do you want to do?"

I lean back to look him in the eyes. "I want to get this guy."

He smiles. "So, you're all tough now?"

And I realize that I actually do feel kind of tough. Me. *I* solved the mystery. *I* ran after the bad guy. Sure, maybe I was the last to get here, but it was me who had the idea to move the crates to flush Kris out.

Maybe I really am tough. Maybe I should get those bright blue highlights Sammi was talking about. Then I might even be approaching badass territory.

"What's the plan?" Tyson whispers.

"We just . . . push." I shrug. It's not much of a plan, but it worked before, and I'm amped to see it work again. So amped, in fact, that I decide to let my runaway mouth do something useful for once. "But first—"

Before I can think any more about it, I lean into him and press my lips to his. I kiss him like I actually know what I'm doing. Like I've thrown myself at dozens of guys before—or, better yet, like dozens of them have thrown themselves at me. He's startled, but only for a second, and then he responds, cupping the back of my head while his other arm tightens against my back.

With my brain still zinging around in the stratosphere, I pull back. "For luck. Now, come on. Let's catch a bad guy!"

As I climb out of his lap, I'm amazed to realize my cheeks aren't flaming with embarrassment. I can't believe I just kissed him, but now that it's done, I honestly feel more relaxed. Even with him staring at me, looking a little dazed.

We crouch together behind the giant cardboard box on top of the pallet.

"One, two, three," Tyson counts softly, and then we push. The box must be full of something a lot heavier than the empty boxes in the one Sammi and I shoved, because it barely moves. The sound doesn't even penetrate the general din.

I frown. "Okay, that won't work."

"Come on." Tyson skulks away from the box, finding a produce cart nearby. It's empty, so I worry that it'll be too light to make any kind of noise, but when he gives it a serious push, the wheels screech like an angry cat and it slams into another nearby pallet.

"That'll do," I whisper as we duck back behind another box.

"Come on out, Kris!" shouts Harper again. "We've already called for backup. You're not going to get away. Why not cooperate?"

In the distance, I hear another loud crash, and grin at Tyson.

"This is nuts," he whispers.

"Let's go." I sneak back the way I came from, making my way toward the back entrance as best I can. Movement on the left makes me pause, but then I see a flash of long black hair and realize Zaina is rolling one of the big towering carts filled with milk. She gets it wedged between two crates, making that particular path impassible. It's like a barricade.

Then I see Sammi doing the same a little farther down.

Then comes another loud crash from the other side of the room. Gabe's laughter rings out.

"Kris, don't be stupid!" Harper shouts. Does he even know we're in the room with him? I wonder where Reyes is, and if there really is backup on the way. I hope so.

A few more thumps and crashes ring out, and suddenly I spot Kris. He's only about ten feet away from me, but moving away, toward the back wall. The loading docks are back there, with their giant garage doors closed. I have no idea how they open, or if they're locked in some way, but I don't want him to get close enough to try one.

Without a second thought, I stand up, and call out as loud as I can, "He's at the loading dock!"

I don't know exactly what happens next, because Tyson grabs me by the arm and yanks me down hard enough to make me yelp in pain. There's some shouting and a long chattering sound, then Harper's voice and the static of his radio.

"Reyes, I've got him. In the storage area. Loading dock."

## FICTIONAL CHARACTERS I NOW OFFICIALLY RESEMBLE

Velma

Nancy Drew

Veronica Mars

Sherlock Holmes

"I can't believe how dumb you are," Sammi says as we gather our stuff from our lockers. She's said it three times already. It's the first time one of her insults has given me a little glow of pride.

I shrug. "I didn't want him to get away."

"What if he'd had a gun?" Tyson says.

"You guys are the ones who ran after him in the first place," I point out.

"We weren't even sure he did anything wrong," he retorts.

"Yeah, because innocent people usually run away from the cops," Gabe says.

I point to Gabe. "Exactly. That's what I was thinking."

"You were not." Sammi rolls her eyes.

I smile. I'm giddy, like I just hopped down from the summit of Everest.

"I still can't believe Kris stole the money," Micah says.

"I know," I agree. "He was always so nice. I never would have guessed."

"It's always the ones you least suspect," Gabe says.

"He's not that nice," Zaina reminds us.

I glance at her, but her face doesn't show any emotion.

"Look on the bright side, Z," Sammi says. "Dude got tased. He probably pissed himself."

"I can't believe he blamed us," Tyson says. Solomon told us that the reason we'd all been detained at the store was that Kris had told him privately that he had reason to believe it was one of us.

"Asshole," Sammi said.

"I just can't believe Solomon believed him," Zaina says.

"He *is* the owner's son," I remind her. "I'm sure Mr. Solomon was thinking about his job."

"But why *us*?" Tyson says.

"He was probably trying to buy himself time to make a getaway," Gabe reasoned. "Maybe he figured nothing would happen to us since he knew for a fact we hadn't done it."

"And he probably thought it wouldn't matter what happened to us since we're minors," I add.

"I'm not," Gabe says. "What a jerk."

"What I don't understand," Zaina says, "is why he stayed here at the store after it was closed. He knew he stole the money. Why would he stay?"

"Because I asked him to." Mr. Solomon startles us all, speaking from the door to the Manager's Office. "I thought it would be helpful for you all to have a familiar face."

"I can't believe he stayed," Gabe says.

"Well, obviously he's not the sharpest tool in the shed." Sammi crosses her arms. "He stole a bunch of charity money from his own father's company."

"And kept marked bills in his pocket," I say.

Solomon sighs. "He always seemed like a good employee. This is quite a blow."

"Sorry, Mr. Solomon," Micah says.

"I'm the one who should be sorry," he says. "I shouldn't have kept you here on one person's word. It's Christmas Eve, for heaven's sake."

"It's all right," Gabe says.

"I know this won't make up for keeping you here, but why don't you each take something from the bakery for your families? My treat."

There are general sounds of agreement and thanks, and he smiles.

"I'll go turn the lights on in that area."

I wind my scarf around my neck. "Thanks again for taking care of me earlier, you guys."

"No problem." Tyson hooks his thumbs in his pockets and gives me a look that reminds me of my mother when she doesn't approve of something. "Just don't ever try to hide that stuff from us again."

"Yeah, really," Gabe agrees.

"We don't want you to get sick," Zaina says.

"I'm sorry. I just . . . people act weird when they find out."

"People *are* weird," Sammi says.

"Well, you are." Gabe knocks her gently with his elbow. She shakes her head at him. "Remind me to kick your ass later."

"You'll have to catch me first." He goes into a low stance, like he's guarding her in basketball, dodging from side to side while she stands still, regarding him with amusement.

"Come on, hero, let's go get some free cake."

They walk ahead of the rest of us as we go toward the bakery to meet Solomon. Tyson carries my mom's ham for me, which slows him down. I hang back with him—it's my ham, after all—but after a second, he catches me by the elbow to slow me until the others are practically out of sight. I look at him, curious.

"Before, in the cooler?" he says.

The familiar feeling of heat rushes into my face. So I guess my journey toward general badassery isn't quite complete. I swallow hard. "Yeah, about that. I know you probably didn't want me to—you know. It was just—"

"Why would you think that?" he interrupts, looking 100 percent confused.

"Wait . . . what?" The others are around the corner now, leaving us alone in the dark Produce department. It smells like apples and damp cardboard.

He shakes his head and shifts the ham under one arm, freeing up a hand to push his glasses up. "What I was trying to say before was that I liked it."

Self-conscious, I look down, but I can't help smiling. "Really?"

"Except—"

Oh no. All the heat drains from my face in an instant.

He shifts to lower the ham to the floor. "—I should have done it first."

My heart roars to life again. "Yeah?"

He catches my arm by the elbow and pulls me closer. Then he slides his arms around my waist and bends to kiss me.

It's so much better not sitting on the floor of a cold storage warehouse. I struggle to keep my knees from buckling as every nerve in my body sizzles and jumps.

Tyson doesn't kiss me for long, but my head is spinning when he stops. I look up at him, giggling for no good reason.

"So, do you want a ride home?" I ask.

He smiles. "Definitely."

"Okay, but you have to carry the ham."

He laughs. "As you wish."

## TOP TEN WEIRDEST THINGS TO EVER HAPPEN IN GOODFOODS MARKET*

(As compiled by Chloe Novak, Tyson Scott, Micah Yoder, Sammi Baker, Zaina Malak, and Gabe Rossi)

10. When a group of people dressed like vampires came in and bought a bunch of meat.

9. The guy who tried to hold up one of the cashiers, but accidentally showed that his "gun" was actually a squirt gun so another customer just grabbed him.

8. The man who came in dressed in a silver suit, said he was from the future, and demanded to know where we kept the nutrition tablets.

7. The man who paid his entire grocery bill—$215.56—in coins.

6. The stocker who quit in the middle of his shift after setting off a cherry bomb in a gallon of milk.

5. The woman who put her dog in a dress and drove her around the store sitting in the child seat. And when Kris tried to enforce the "No Dogs" policy, she claimed he was a service dog that helped her with her depression.
4. The customer who slapped the other shift manager, Randy, in the face.
3. When Gabe assaulted the Salvation Army bell ringer.
2. The woman who ate chips and dip in the bathroom stall, then gave half a bottle of peppermint schnapps to Sammi.
1. The time Kris stole all the charity money, blamed us, ran from the cops on Christmas Eve, and we all saved the day.
   *A work in progress

A few hours ago, I would have paid good money to be outside the building and ready to head home. Now, I feel almost reluctant to leave everyone.

Tyson is coming with me, of course, and he stands beside me with my ham under one arm, and his other hand against my back. I like the way it feels there, even if the slight contact makes it hard to concentrate.

Micah and Zaina, neither of whom drove, both need rides. Sammi is going to take Micah home, and Gabe's taking Zaina.

This morning, I would never have imagined Sammi submitting to being in an enclosed space with Micah for the entirety of a car ride. It has definitely been a strange day.

And still we all linger in the lot, despite the frigid air. The frozen rain cleared off at some point, leaving the sky a deep, velvety black, pinpointed with stars. Our breathing makes cloud after cloud of vapor that fades into the dark.

"It's a good night to look for Santa Claus," I say, thinking of younger years when I'd spent Christmas Eve craning my neck at the sky.

"My sister must be loving this," Micah says.

That makes me think of my brother, home from college, and my mother, probably wringing her hands with worry over what, if anything, I've eaten since I left this morning. Not to mention the whereabouts of her ham. When I tell her about the day, I'm definitely going to leave out the part where I almost passed out from low blood sugar.

"I should go," I say at last.

"We all should," Tyson agrees.

We say good-bye to one another. A few Merry Christmases drift over the roofs of the cars as we open doors. Micah asks when everyone is working again and we tell him. No one is working tomorrow, obviously, and only Tyson and Sammi are on the day after that. I feel a strange sense of loneliness thinking of not seeing these people again for a while.

Tyson knows the deal with my car from previous rides home, so he gets in first and reaches across to release the latch on my side. It's nice not to crawl across the front. When I turn the engine over, I smile at him, and he reaches out to squeeze my hand. Even with gloves on, the warmth of his palm reaches mine and I feel the urge to giggle again.

Instead, I have to take my hand back for a moment to back out of my parking space. Gabe is the first in line with Sammi queued behind him to pull out of the lot, but the brake lights on Gabe's car are still lit. Suddenly, the door opens and he gets out.

My finger finds the switch to let my window down, wondering what Gabe has to say, but he stops at Sammi's window first and taps on it until she rolls it down.

It's hard to hear anything from where we're idling, but it's not hard to figure out what's happening when Gabe leans in the window. My headlights catch their silhouettes as she turns her head slightly. They are unmistakably kissing.

"Oh my God!" My glasses slide down my nose as I whip my head to look at Tyson. "Did you see that?"

"I saw."

"What did—when did—wha . . . ?" I stammer.

Gabe pulls back, resting his elbows on the window frame for a second. He smiles, nods, gives a little salute to Micah, and straightens up. Holding up a hand to block the glare of my headlights from his eyes, he trots toward us.

My window is already down, so he just bends slightly to look through the opening at us.

"So, I'm thinking we should probably hang out. You guys wanna come by my house? Maybe the day after tomorrow? When Tyce and Sammi are done with work?"

It's the last thing I expected. "Um . . . sure."

"Gimme your number," he says. "I'll text you the address." He opens his phone and hands it to me to type in my info.

I do, even though I'm still a little stunned, and pass it to Tyson.

Tyson takes the phone, but ducks to look at him. "What the hell was that?" He points to Sammi's car.

Gabe shrugs. "Just something I had to do."

"But—" I start, but I can't finish. I have no idea what to say.

Tyson makes a dismissive sound, but types in his number and hands the phone back to Gabe.

"Merry Christmas, you guys," he says.

"Merry Christmas," I say, my mind still running on autopilot.

He jogs back to his own car, thumping his fist lightly on Sammi's window as he passes her. I strain to see her through the rear window, but she's too hidden behind the headrest. I can't see Micah, either.

"That was . . . weird," Tyson says.

"You could say that." I nod, watching the brake lights dim as Gabe puts his car into gear and cruises away from the lot. Sammi is quick to follow, her car going in the opposite direction.

"What the hell went down in that cooler today?" he wonders.

"I have no idea."

"Weird."

"So, like, are we all going to be friends now?" I ask.

Tyson reaches across to take my hand again. "I don't know. Maybe. Might be worth a try, right?"

I think about that.

I think about Sammi's attitude, and Micah's naive genius, and Zaina's shyness. I think of how they all rallied to take care of me, and how none of them treated me any different when it was over. I think of how lonely I've been since I started at my new school. I think about how I don't really want to leave, even after all these hours together. Even with my family waiting at home.

I think a lot about Tyson, and how he kissed me the second time, and how maybe I hadn't been so off base with my crush after all. I think about the way I've never told my parents I take Tyson home sometimes, knowing they'd worry about me driving around someone they didn't know, about the "bad" parts of town that are so much closer to his neighborhood than mine, about me being alone with a boy of any kind.

I think I'm going to have to tell them about him when I get home. Him and all of it. They're not going to be thrilled at first, but maybe they'll see that I can take care of myself after all.

Maybe things can finally change. At least a little bit. Maybe I can finally stop being their precious, broken baby girl.

It's worth a try, right?

"Yeah, I think it is," I say finally.

"Me too," Tyson says.

When I pull up to the curb outside Tyson's house, he leans across, cupping my cheek to pull me close and kiss me once more. And if it took being under pseudoarrest in a grocery store on Christmas Eve for that to happen, it was all worth it.

## THINGS THAT ARE BETTER THAN KISSING TYSON SCOTT
1. Kissing him again

# ACKNOWLEDGMENTS

TOP TEN THANK-YOUS TO EVERYONE WHO KEPT ME SANE AND/OR PROVIDED A HELMET AND COOKIES WHEN SANE WASN'T ATTAINABLE

1. My editor, Erica Sussman, who somehow knew what I was trying to do even though my first efforts were so far off, they might as well have been written in hieroglyphics. Thanks also to the entire team at HarperTeen, including Tyler Infinger, the wonderfully crazy people on the Epic Reads team, the art department, which is full of geniuses, and the entire marketing team, especially Alison Lisnow.

2. Laura Bradford, super agent, for being the savvy one so I can live in blissful naïveté.

3. The earliest inklings of this story were nurtured into a workable idea through a careful combination of grocery store experience, enthusiasm, and helpless laughter by the lovely Jessica Souders, who did it all behind the wheel of a rental car with the world's stupidest GPS.

4. Heather Whitley helped me find the way, as ever. Even when I forget to email her back because I keep my brain in a colander when I'm not using it.

5. The Wednesday Night Barnes & Noble Crew bore witness

to much head-to-keyboard and face-smushing anxiety. Thank you, ladies, for telling me I could do it anyway, especially Jill Brevers, Barb Britton, Liz Kreger, Liz Lincoln, Karen Miller, Betsy Norman, and Sandee Turriff.

6. The Class of 2k14 (Varsha Bajaj, Kate Bassett, Rebecca Behrens, Crystal Chan, Stephanie Diaz, Stefanie Gaither, Tracy Holczer, Christine Kohler, Melissa Landers, R. C. Lewis, Lauren Magaziner, Nicole Maggi, Elizabeth May, Amy K. Nichols, Kristin Rae, Gayle Rosengren, Lisa Ann Scott, Carmella Van Vleet, Amy Zhang) provided invaluable support, sympathy, and cheerleading.

7. My earliest readers include Cathy Weishan; Lindsay, Mary, and Evan Maruszewski; Sarah Horne; and Anne Williams. You guys are the best cheerleaders around.

8. To everyone who gave me insight into the fascinating world of grocery stores and shared all their tales of weirdness in retail. Be nice to the people who work where you shop, you guys. Seriously.

9. The basic layout of my fictionalized GoodFoods owes itself almost entirely to my local grocery store, Metro Market. I'd like to give a special thank-you to the hardworking crew of the store who just kept smiling as I stood on tiptoe, peering into the Employees Only sections, eavesdropping on conversations, and just generally being a creeper. You guys are

awesome for not throwing me out. And for your cookies. Your cookies are the fricking best thing on Earth.

10. To my amazing family. We survived another one, you guys! Thanks for putting up with strange questions, my vacant stare, and the poor quality of housekeeping. I couldn't do this without you, even if you don't always know that.